LAWRENCE BLOCK
TIME TO MURDER AND CREATE

TIME TO MURDER AND CREATE

A Jove Book / published by arrangement with
the author

PRINTING HISTORY
Dell edition / January 1977
Jove edition / February 1983

ISBN: 0–515–06801–2

PRINTED IN THE UNITED STATES OF AMERICA

Therefore was a single man only first created, to teach thee that whosoever destroyeth a single soul from the children of man, Scripture charges him as though he had destroyed the whole world.

—THE TALMUD

CHAPTER ONE

For seven consecutive Fridays I got telephone calls from him. I wasn't always there to receive them. It didn't matter, because he and I had nothing to say to each other. If I was out when he called, there would be a message slip in my box when I got back to the hotel. I would glance at it and throw it away and forget about it.

Then, on the second Friday in April, he didn't call. I spent the evening around the corner at Armstrong's, drinking bourbon and coffee and watching a couple of interns fail to impress a couple of nurses. The place thinned out early for a Friday, and around two Trina went home and Billie locked the door to keep Ninth Avenue outside. We had a couple of drinks and talked about the Knicks and how it all depended on Willis Reed. At a quarter of three I took my coat off the peg and went home.

No messages.

It didn't have to mean anything. Our arrangement was that he would call every Friday to let me know he was alive. If I was there to catch his call, we would say hello to each other. Otherwise he'd leave a message: *Your laundry is ready*. But he could have forgotten or he could be drunk or almost anything.

I got undressed and into bed and lay on my side looking out the window. There's an office building ten or twelve blocks downtown where they leave the lights on at night. You can gauge the pollution level fairly accurately by how much the lights appear to flicker. They were not only flickering wildly that night, they even had a yellow cast to them.

I rolled over and closed my eyes and thought about the phone call that hadn't come. I decided he hadn't forgotten and he wasn't drunk.

The Spinner was dead.

They called him the Spinner because of a habit he had. He carried an old silver dollar as a good-luck charm, and he would haul it out of his pants pocket all the time, prop it up on a table top with his left forefinger, then cock his right middle finger and give the edge of the coin a flick. If he was talking to you, his eyes would stay on the spinning coin while he spoke, and he seemed to be directing his words as much to the dollar as to you.

I had last witnessed this performance on a weekday afternoon in early February. He found me at my usual corner table in Armstrong's. He was dressed Broadway sharp: a pearl-gray suit with a lot of flash, a dark-gray monogrammed shirt, a silk tie the same color as the shirt, a pearl tie tack. He was wearing a pair of those platform shoes that give you an extra inch and a half or so. They boosted his height to maybe five six, five seven. The coat over his arm was navy blue and looked like cashmere.

"Matthew Scudder," he said. "You look the same, and how long has it been?"

"A couple of years."

"Too damn long." He put his coat on an empty chair, settled a slim attaché case on top of it, and placed a narrow-brimmed gray hat on top of the attaché case. He seated himself across the table from me and dug his lucky charm out of his pocket. I watched him set it spinning. "Too goddamned long, Matt," he told the coin.

"You're looking good, Spinner."

"Been havin' a nice run of luck."

"That's always good."

"Long as it keeps runnin'."

Trina came over, and I ordered another cup of coffee and a shot of bourbon. Spinner turned to her and worked his narrow little face into a quizzical frown. "Gee, I don't know," he said. "Do you suppose I could have a glass of milk?"

She said he could and went away to fetch it. "I can't drink no more," he said. "It's this fuckin' ulcer."

"They tell me it goes with success."

"It goes with aggravation is what it goes with. Doc gave me a list of what I can't eat. Everything I like is on it. I got it aced, I can go to the best restaurants and then I can order myself a plate of fuckin' cottage cheese."

He picked up the dollar and gave it a spin.

I had known him over the years while I was on the force. He'd been picked up maybe a dozen times, always on minor things, but he'd never done any time. He always managed to buy his way off the hook, with either money or information. He set me up for a good collar, a receiver of stolen goods, and another time he gave us a handle on a homicide case. In between he would peddle us information, trading something he'd overheard for a ten- or twenty-dollar bill. He was small and unimpressive and he knew the right moves and a lot of people were stupid enough to talk in his presence.

He said, "Matt, I didn't just happen to walk in here off the street."

"I had that feeling."

"Yeah." The dollar started to wobble, and he snatched it up. He had very quick hands. We always figured him for a sometime pickpocket, but I don't think anybody ever nailed him for it. "The thing is, I got problems."

"They go with ulcers, too."

"You bet your ass they do." Spin. "What it is, I got something I want you to hold for me."

"Oh?"

He took a sip of milk. He put the glass down and reached over to drum his fingers against the attaché case. "I got an envelope in here. What I want is for you to hold on to it for me. Put it some place safe where nobody's gonna run across it, you know?"

"What's in the envelope?"

He gave his head an impatient little shake. "Part of it is you don't have to know what's in the envelope."

"How long do I have to hold it?"

"Well, that's the whole thing." Spin. "See, lots of things can happen to a person. I could walk out, step off the curb, get hit by the Ninth Avenue bus. All the things that can happen to a person, I mean, you just never know."

"Is somebody trying for you, Spinner?"

The eyes came up to meet mine, then dropped quickly. "It could be," he said.

"You know who?"

"I don't even know if, never mind who." Wobble, snatch. Spin.

"The envelope's your insurance."

"Something like that."

I sipped coffee. I said, "I don't know if I'm right for this, Spinner. The usual thing, you take your envelope to a lawyer and work out a set of instructions. He tosses it into a safe and that's it."

"I thought of that."

"So?"

"No point to it. The kind of lawyers I know, the minute I walk out of their office they got the fuckin' envelope open. A straight lawyer, he's gonna run his eyes over me and go out and wash his hands."

"Not necessarily."

"There's something else. Say I get hit by a bus, then the lawyer would only have to get the envelope to you. This way we cut out the middleman, right?"

"Why do I have to wind up with the envelope?"

"You'll find out when you open it. *If* you open it."

"Everything's very roundabout, isn't it?"

"Everything's very tricky lately, Matt. Ulcers and aggravation."

"And better clothes than I ever saw you wear in your life."

"Yeah, they can fuckin' bury me in 'em." Spin. "Look, all you gotta do is take the envelope, you stick it in a safe-deposit box, something, somewhere, that's up to you."

"Suppose *I* get hit by a bus?"

He thought it over and we worked it out. The envelope would go under the rug in my hotel room. If I died suddenly, Spinner could come around and retrieve his property. He wouldn't need a key. He'd never needed one in the past.

We worked out details, the weekly phone call, the bland message if I wasn't in. I ordered another drink. Spinner still had plenty of milk left.

I asked him why he had picked me.

"Well, you were always straight with me, Matt. You been off the force how long? A couple of years?"

"Something like that."

"Yeah, you quit. I'm not good on the details. You killed some kid or something?"

"Yeah. Line of duty, a bullet took a bad hop."

"Catch a lot of static from on top?"

I looked at my coffee and thought about it. A summer night, the heat almost visible in the air, the air conditioning working overtime in the Spectacle, a bar in Washington Heights where a cop got his drinks on the house. I was off duty, except you never really are, and two kids picked that night to hold up the place. They shot the bartender dead on their way out. I chased them into the street, killed one of them, splintered the other one's thigh bone.

But one shot was off and took a richochet that bounced it right into the eye of a seven-year-old girl named Estrellita Rivera. Right in the eye, and through soft tissue and on into the brain.

"I was out of line," the Spinner said. "I shouldn'ta brought it up."

"No, that's all right. I didn't get any static. I got a commendation, as a matter of fact. There was a hearing, and I was completely exonerated."

"And then you quit the force."

"I sort of lost my taste for the work. And for other things. A house on the Island. A wife. My sons."

"I guess it happens," he said.

"I guess it does."

"So what you're doing, you're sort of a private cop, huh?"

I shrugged. "I don't have a license. Sometimes I do favors for people and they pay me for it."

"Well, getting back to our little business . . ." Spin. "You'd be doing me a favor is what you'd be doing."

"If you think so."

He picked up the dollar in mid-spin, looked at it, set it down on the blue-and-white checkered tablecloth.

I said, "You don't want to get killed, Spinner."

"Fuck, no."

"Can't you get out from under?"

"Maybe. Maybe not. Let's don't talk about that part of it, huh?"

"Whatever you say."

" 'Cause if somebody wants to kill you, what the fuck can you do about it? Nothin'."

"You're probably right."

"You'll handle this for me, Matt?"

"I'll hang on to your envelope. I'm not saying what I'll do if I have to open it, because I don't know what's in it."

"If it happens, then you'll know."

"No guarantees I'll do it, whatever it is."

He took a long look at me, reading something in my face that I didn't know was there. "You'll do it," he said.

"Maybe."

"You'll do it. And if you don't I won't know about it, so what the fuck. Listen, what do you want in front?"

"I don't know what it is I'm supposed to do."

"I mean for keeping the envelope. How much do you want?"

I never know how to set fees. I thought for a moment. I said, "That's a nice suit you're wearing."

"Huh? Thanks."

"Where'd you get it?"

"Phil Kronfeld's. Over on Broadway?"

"I know where it is."

"You really like it?"

"It looks good on you. What did it set you back?"

"Three twenty."

"Then that's my fee."

"You want the fuckin' suit?"

"I want three hundred and twenty dollars."

"*Oh.*" He tossed his head, amused. "You had me goin' there for a minute. I couldn't understand what the fuck you'd want with the suit."

"I don't think it would fit."

"I guess not. Three twenty? Yeah, I guess that's as good a number as any." He got out a fat alligator wallet and counted out six fifties and a twenty. "Three—two—oh," he said, handing them to me. "If this drags on and on and you want more, you let me know. Good enough?"

"Good enough. Suppose I have to get in touch with you, Spinner?"

"Uh-uh."

"Okay."

"Like, you won't have to, and if I wanted to give you an address I couldn't anyway."

"Okay."

He opened the attaché and passed me a nine-by-twelve manila envelope sealed on both ends with heavy-duty tape. I took it from him and put it on the bench beside me. He gave the silver dollar a spin, picked it up, put it in his pocket, and beckoned to Trina for the check. I let him have it. He paid it and left a two-dollar tip.

"What's so funny, Matt?"

"Just that I never saw you grab a check before. And I've seen you pick up other people's tips."

"Well, things change."

"I guess they do."

"I didn't do that often, dragging down somebody's tips. You do lots of things when you're hungry."

"Sure."

He got to his feet, hesitated, put out his hand. I shook it. He turned to go, and I said, "Spinner?"

"What?"

"You said the kind of lawyers you know would open the envelope as soon as you left the office."

"You bet your ass they would."

"How come you don't think I will?"

He looked at me as though the question was a stupid one. "You're honest," he said.

"Oh, Christ. You know I used to take. I let you buy your way out of a collar or two, for Christ's sake."

"Yeah, but you were always square with me. There's honest and there's honest. You're not gonna open that envelope until you have to."

I knew he was right. I just didn't know how he knew it. "Take care of yourself," I said.

"Yeah, you too."

"Watch yourself crossing the street."

"Huh?"

"Watch out for buses."

He laughed a little, but I don't think he thought it was funny.

Later that day, I stopped off at a church and stuffed thirty-two dollars into the poor box. I sat in a rear pew and thought about the Spinner. He'd given me easy money. All I had to do to earn it was nothing at all.

Back in my room, I rolled up the rug and put Spinner's envelope beneath it, centering it under the bed. The maid runs the vacuum cleaner occasionally but never moves the furniture around. I put the rug back in place and promptly forgot about the envelope, and every Friday a call or a message would assure me that Spinner was alive and the envelope could stay right where it was.

CHAPTER TWO

For the next three days I read the papers twice a day and waited for a phone call. Monday night I picked up the early edition of the *Times* on the way to my room. Under the heading of "Metropolitan Briefs" there's always a batch of crime items tagged "From the Police Blotter," and the last one was the one I was looking for. An unidentified male, white, height approximately five six, weight approximately one forty, age approximately forty-five, had been fished out of the East River with a crushed skull.

It sounded right. I'd have put his age a few years higher and his weight a few pounds lower, but otherwise it sounded very right. I couldn't know that it was Spinner. I couldn't even know that the man, whoever he was, had been murdered. The skull damage could have been done after he went into the water. And there was nothing in the item to indicate how long he'd been in the water. If it was more than ten days or so, it wasn't Spinner; I'd heard from him the Friday before.

I looked at my watch. It wasn't too late to call someone, but it was far too late to call someone and

11

seem casual about it. And it was too early to open his envelope. I didn't want to do that until I was very certain he was dead.

I had a couple more drinks than usual, because sleep was a long time coming. In the morning I woke up with a headache and a bad taste in my mouth. I used aspirin and mouthwash and went down to the Red Flame for breakfast. I picked up a later *Times*, but there was nothing further on the floater. They had the same item as the earlier edition.

Eddie Koehler is a lieutenant now, attached to the Sixth Precinct in the West Village. I called from my room and managed to get through to him. "Hey, Matt," he said. "It's been a while."

It hadn't been all that long. I asked about his family and he asked about mine. "They're fine," I said.

"You could always go back there," he said.

I couldn't, for far more reasons than I wanted to go into. I couldn't start carrying a badge again, either, but that didn't keep him from asking his next question.

"I don't suppose you're ready to rejoin the human race, huh?"

"That's not going to happen, Eddie."

"Instead you got to live in a dump and scrounge for every buck. Listen, you want to drink yourself to death, that's your business."

"That's right."

"But what's the sense paying for your own drinks when you can drink free? You were born to be a cop, Matt."

"The reason I called—"

"Yeah, there has to be a reason, doesn't there?"

I waited for a minute. Then I said, "Something in

the paper that caught my eye, and I thought maybe you could save me a trip to the morgue. They took a floater out of the East River yesterday. Little guy, middle-aged."

"So?"

"Could you find out if they identified him yet?"

"Probably. What's your interest?"

"I got a missing husband I'm sort of looking for. He fits the description. I could go down and take a look at him, but I only know him from photographs and after a little while in the water—"

"Yeah, right. What's your guy's name and I'll find out."

"Let's do it the other way around," I said. "It's supposed to be confidential, I don't want to spread the name if I don't have to."

"I guess I could make a couple of calls."

"If it's my guy, you'll get yourself a hat."

"I figured as much. And if it's not?"

"You'll get my sincere gratitude."

"Fuck you too," he said. "I hope it's your guy. I can use a hat. Hey, that's funny, come to think of it."

"How?"

"You're looking for a guy and I'm hoping he's dead. You think about it, it's pretty funny."

The phone rang forty minutes later. He said, "It's a shame, I could've used a hat."

"They didn't get a make?"

"Oh, they got a make, they made him on fingerprints, but he's not a guy anybody's gonna hire you to look for. He's a character, we got a sheet on him a yard long. You must've run into him once or twice yourself."

"What's his name?"

"Jacob Jablon. Did a little stooling, a little boosting, all kinds of dumb shit."

"Name's familiar."

"They called him the Spinner."

"I did know him," I said. "Haven't run into him in years. He used to spin a silver dollar all the time."

"Well, all he's gonna spin now is in his grave."

I drew a breath. I said, "He's not my guy."

"I didn't think so. I don't think he was anybody's husband, and if he was she wouldn't want him found."

"It's not the wife who's looking for my guy."

"It's not?"

"It's his girlfriend."

"I'll be a son of a bitch."

"And I don't think he's in town in the first place, but I might as well string her for a few bucks. A guy wants to disappear, he's just going to do it."

"That's the way it generally goes, but if she wants to hand you money—"

"That's my feeling," I said. "How long was the Spinner in the water? Do they know that yet?"

"I think they said four, five days. What's your interest?"

"Getting him on prints, I figured it had to be fairly recent."

"Oh, prints'll hold a week, easy. Longer sometimes, depending on the fish. Imagine fingerprinting a floater—shit, if I did that I'd be a long time before I wanted anything to eat. Imagine doing the autopsy."

"Well, that shouldn't be hard. Somebody must have hit him on the head."

"Considering who he was, I'd say there's no question. He wasn't the type to go swimming and accidentally hit his head on a pier. What'll you bet they don't come up with a conclusive homicide tag for it, though?"

"Why's that?"

"Because they don't want this sitting in the open file for the next fifty years, and who wants to bust their balls finding out what happened to an asshole like the Spinner? So he's dead, so nobody's gonna cry for him."

"I always got along with him."

"He was a cheap little crook. Whoever bumped him did the world a favor."

"I suppose you're right."

I got the manila envelope out from under the rug. The tape didn't want to budge, so I got my penknife from the dresser and slit the envelope open along the fold. Then I just sat on the edge of the bed with the envelope in my hand for a few minutes.

I didn't really want to know what was in it.

After a while I opened it, and I spent the next three hours in my room going over the contents. They answered a few questions, but not nearly as many as they asked. Finally I put everything back in the envelope and returned it to its place under the rug.

The cops would sweep Spinner Jablon under the rug, and that's what I wanted to do with his envelope. There were a lot of things I could do, and what I most wanted to do was nothing at all, so until my options had time to sort themselves out in my head the envelope could stay in its hiding place.

I stretched out on the bed with a book, but after I'd gone through a few pages I realized I was reading without paying attention. And my little room was beginning to feel even smaller than usual. I went out and walked around for a while, and then I hit a few places and had a few drinks. I started out in Polly's Cage, across the street from the hotel, then Kilcullen's, then Spiro and Antares. Somewhere along the way I stopped at a deli for a couple of sandwiches. I wound up in Armstrong's, and I was still there when Trina ended her shift. I told her to sit down and I'd buy her a drink.

"But just one, Matt. I got places to go, people to see."

"So do I, but I don't want to go there and I don't want to see them."

"You could be just the slightest bit drunk."

"It's not impossible."

I went to the bar and got our drinks. Plain bourbon for me, a vodka and tonic for her. I came back to the table, and she picked up her glass.

She said, "To crime?"

"You've really only got time for one?"

"I don't even have time for the one, but one's got to be the limit."

"Then let's not make it to crime. Let's make it absent friends."

CHAPTER THREE

I suppose I had a fair idea what was in the envelope before I opened it. When a man who sidesteps through life by keeping his ears open suddenly turns up wearing a three-hundred-dollar suit, it's not hard to figure out how he got it. After a lifetime of selling information, the Spinner had come up with something too good to sell. Instead of peddling information, he had turned to peddling silence. Blackmailers are richer than stool pigeons, because their commodity is not a one-time thing; they can rent it out to the same person over and over for a lifetime.

The only problem is that their lifetimes tend to shrink. The Spinner became a bad actuarial risk the day he got successful. First aggravation and ulcers, then a dented skull and a long swim.

A blackmailer needs insurance. He has to have some leverage that will convince his victim not to terminate the blackmail by terminating the blackmailer. Somebody—a lawyer, a girlfriend, anyone—sits in the background with whatever evidence has the victim squirming in the first place. If the blackmailer dies, the evidence goes to the cops and the shit hits

17

the fan. Every blackmailer makes a point of letting the victim know about this added element. Sometimes there's no confederate, no envelope to be mailed, because evidence lying around is dangerous to all concerned, so the blackmailer just *says* that there is and figures the mark won't call his bluff. Sometimes the mark believes him, and sometimes he doesn't.

Spinner Jablon probably told his mark about the magic envelope from the beginning. But in February he had started to sweat. He had decided that somebody was trying to kill him, or was likely to try, so he had put his envelope together. An actual envelope wouldn't keep him alive if the idea of the envelope failed. He'd be just as dead, and he had known it.

But he had been, in the final analysis, a pro. Penny-ante for almost all his life, but professional just the same. And a professional doesn't get mad. He gets even.

He'd had a problem, though, and it became my problem when I cut his envelope open and checked its contents. Because Spinner had known that he would have to get even with somebody.

He just hadn't known who.

The first thing I looked at was the letter. It was typed, which suggested that at one time or another he had stolen one more typewriter than he could sell, so he'd kept it around. He hadn't used it a hell of a lot. His letter was full of xxxxxx'd out words and phrases, skips between letters, and enough misspelled words to make it interesting. But it added up to something like this:

Matt:

    If you're reading this I'm a dead man. I hope

it blows over but no bets on that. I think somebody tried for me yesterday. There was this car just about crawled up the curb coming at me.

What I got going is blackmail. I fell into some information worth good money. Years of scrounging around and I finally stepped right into it.

There is three of them. You'll see how it lays when you open the other envelopes. That is the problem, the three of them, because if I'm dead one of them did it and I don't know which. I got each one on a string and I don't know which one I'm choking.

This Prager, two years ago December his daughter ran down a kid on a tricycle and kept on going on account of she was driving on a suspended license and strung out on speed and grass and I don't know what else. Prager has more money than God and he spread it on everybody and his kid was never picked up. All the information is in the envelope. He was the first one, I overheard some shit in a bar and I fed this one guy drinks and he opened up for me. I'm not taking him for anything he can't afford and he just pays me like you pay rent the first of the month but who knows when a man is going to go crazy and maybe that's what happened. He wants me dead, shit, he could hire it done easy enough.

The Ethridge broad was just dumb luck. I hit on her picture in the newspapers, some society page hype, and I reckonized her from this fuck film I saw some years back. Talk about remembering a face, and who looks at the face, but maybe she was giving head to some dude and it caught in my mind. I read all these schools she went to and I couldn't add it up, so I did some homework, and there was a couple years when she dropped out of sight and went into things a little heavy, and I got pictures and some other shit which you'll see. I been dealing with her and whether her husband knows what's happening or anything else I don't know. She is very hard and could kill a person without turning a hare. You look into her eyes and you know exactly what I mean.

Huysendahl came in third on the string and by this time I'm on the earie as a regular thing because it's all working so nice for me. What I pick up on is his wife is a lezzie. Well this is nothing spectacular Matt as you know. But he's rich as shit and he's thinking about pushing for governor so why not dig a little. The dyke thing is nothing, too many people know it in front, and you spread it around and all that happens is he gets the dyke vote which maybe puts him over the top, so I don't care about that, but why is he still married to this dyke, that's my question. Like is there something kinky about him. So I work my ass to the bone and it turns out there's something there, but getting a handle on it is something else again. He's not a normal queer but his thing is young boys, younger the better. It's a sickness and it is enough to turn your stomach. I got small things, like this kid hospitalized for internal injuries which Huysendahl paid the hospital bills, but I wanted to be able to sink the hook so the pictures were a set up. It don't matter how I set it up but there was other people involved. He must of shit when he saw the pictures. The deal cost me a packet but nobody ever made a better investment.

Matt the thing is if somebody hit me it was one of them, or they hired it out which adds up the same way, and what I want is for you to fuck them good. The one that did it, not the other two which played straight with me, which is why I can't leave this with a lawyer and send it all to the police, because the ones that played straight with me deserve to be off the hook, not to mention if it goes to the wrong cop he just works a shakedown and whoever kills me is home free, except he's still paying out money.

The fourth envelope has your name on it because it is for you. There is 3K in it and that is for you. I don't know if it should be more or what it should be, but there's always the chance you'll just put it in your pocket and shitcan the rest of the stuff, which if it happens I'll be dead and won't know about it. Why I think you'll follow through is something I noticed about you a long time ago, namely that you happen to think there is a difference between murder and other crimes. I am the same. I have done bad things all my life but never killed anybody and never would. I have known people who have killed which I've known for a fact or a rumor and would never get close to them. It is the way I am and I think you are that way too and that is why you might do something, and again if you don't I will not know it.

Your Friend,
Jake "Spinner" Jablon

Wednesday morning I got the envelope out from under the carpet and took another long look at the evidence. I got out my notebook and jotted down a few details. I wasn't going to be able to keep the stuff on hand, because if I made any kind of move I would be making myself visible, and my room would no longer be a clever hiding place.

Spinner had nailed them down tight enough. There was very little hard evidence to prove that Henry Prager's daughter Stacy had left the scene of an accident in which three-year-old Michael Litvak was run down and killed, but in this instance hard evidence wasn't necessary. Spinner had the name of the garage where the Prager car had been repaired, the names of the people in the police department and Westchester D.A.'s office who had been reached, and a few other bits and pieces which would do the job. If you handed the whole package to a good investigative reporter, he wouldn't be able to leave it alone.

The material on Beverly Ethridge was more graphic. The pictures alone might not have been enough. There were a couple of four-by-five color prints and half a dozen clips of film running a few frames each. She was clearly identifiable throughout, and there was no question what she was doing. This by itself might not have been so damaging. A lot of the things people do for a lark in their youth can be written off readily enough after a few years have passed, especially in those social circles where every other closet sports a skeleton.

But the Spinner had done his homework, just as he'd said. He traced Mrs. Ethridge, then Beverly Guildhurst, from the time she left Vassar in her junior year. He turned up an arrest in Santa Barbara for prostitution, sentence suspended. There was a narcotics bust in Vegas, thrown out for lack of evidence, with a strong implication that some family money had pulled her ass out of the fire. In San Diego she was working a badger game with a partner who was a known pimp. It went sour one time; she turned state's evidence and picked up another suspension, while her partner pulled one-to-five in Folsom. The only time she served, as far as Spinner had been able to make out, was fifteen days in Oceanside for drunk and disorderly.

Then she came back and married Kermit Ethridge, and if she hadn't gotten her picture in the paper at just the wrong time, she'd have been home free.

The Huysendahl material was hard to take. The documentary evidence was nothing special: the names of some prepubescent boys and the dates on which Ted Huysendahl had allegedly had sexual relations with them, a stat of hospital records indicating that Huysendahl had sprung for treatment of internal injuries and lacerations for one Jeffrey Kramer, age eleven. But the pictures did not leave you with the feeling that you were looking at the people's choice for the next governor of New York State.

There were an even dozen of them, and they portrayed a fairly full repertoire. The worst one showed Huysendahl's partner, a young and slender black boy, with his face contorted in pain while Huysendahl penetrated him anally. The kid was looking straight at the camera in that shot, as in several of the others, and it was certainly possible that the facial expression of agony was nothing but theater, but that possibility wouldn't prevent nine out of ten average citizens from gladly fitting a noose around Huysendahl's neck and hanging him from the nearest lamppost.

CHAPTER FOUR

At four thirty that afternoon I was in a reception room on the twenty-second floor of a glass and steel office building on Park Avenue in the high Forties. The receptionist and I had the room to ourselves. She was behind a U-shaped ebony desk. She was a shade lighter than the desk, and she wore her hair in a tight-cropped Afro. I sat on a vinyl couch the same color as the desk. The small white parson's table beside it was sparsely covered with magazines: *Architectural Forum, Scientific American,* a couple different golf magazines, last week's *Sports Illustrated.* I didn't think any of them would tell me anything I wanted to know, so I left them where they were and looked at the small oil on the far wall. It was an amateurish seascape with a great many small boats cavorting on a turbulent ocean. Men leaned over the sides of the boat in the foreground. They seemed to be vomiting, but it was hard to believe the artist had intended it that way.

"Mrs. Prager painted that," the girl said. "His wife?"

"It's interesting."

"All those in his office, she painted them, too. It must be wonderful to have a talent like that."

"It must be."

"And she never had a lesson in her life."

The receptionist found this more remarkable than I did. I wondered when Mrs. Prager had taken up painting. After her children were grown, I supposed. There were three Prager children: a boy in medical school at the University of Buffalo, a married daughter in California, and the youngest, Stacy. They had all left the nest now, and Mrs. Prager lived in a landlocked house in Rye and painted stormy seascapes.

"He's off the phone now," the girl said. "I didn't get your name, I'm afraid."

"Matthew Scudder," I said.

She buzzed him to announce my presence. I hadn't expected the name would mean anything to him, and it evidently didn't, because she asked me what my visit was in reference to.

"I'm representing the Michael Litvak project."

If that registered, Prager wasn't letting on. She conveyed his continued puzzlement. "The Hit-and-Run Cooperative," I said. "The Michael Litvak project. It's a confidential matter, I'm sure he'll want to see me."

I was sure he wouldn't want to see me at all, actually, but she repeated my words and he couldn't really avoid it. "He'll see you now," she said, and nodded her curly little head at a door marked PRIVATE.

His office was spacious, the far wall all glass with a rather impressive view of a city that looks better the higher up you go. The decor was traditional, in sharp contrast to the harsh modern furnishings of the

reception room. The walls were paneled in dark
wood—individual boards, not the plywood stuff.
The carpet was the color of tawny port wine. There
were a lot of pictures on the walls, all of them
seascapes, all unmistakably the work of Mrs. Henry
Prager.

I had seen his picture in the papers I'd scanned in
the microfilm room at the library. Just head-and-
shoulder shots, but they had prepared me for a larger
man than the one who now stood up behind the
broad leather-topped desk. And the face in the Bach-
rach photo had beamed with calm assurance. Now it
was lined with apprehension pinned in place by cau-
tion. I approached the desk, and we stood looking
each other over. He seemed to be considering
whether or not to offer his hand. He decided against
it.

He said, "Your name is Scudder?"

"That's right."

"I'm not sure what you want."

Neither was I. There was a red leather chair with
wooden arms near the desk. I pulled it up and sat in it
while he was still on his feet. He hesitated a moment,
then seated himself. I waited for a few seconds on the
off chance that he might have something to say. But
he was pretty good at waiting.

I said, "I mentioned a name before. Michael Litvak."

"I don't know the name."

"Then I'll mention another. Jacob Jablon."

"I don't know that name, either."

"Don't you? Mr. Jablon was an associate of mine.
We did some business together."

"What kind of business would that be?"

"Oh, a little of this, a little of that. Nothing as successful as your line of work, I'm afraid. You're an architectural consultant?"

"That's correct."

"Large-scale projects. Housing developments, office buildings, that sort of thing."

"That's hardly classified information, Mr. Scudder."

"It must pay well."

He looked at me.

"Actually, the phrase you just used. 'Classified information.' That's what I really wanted to talk to you about."

"Oh?"

"My associate Mr. Jablon had to leave town abruptly."

"I don't see how—"

"He retired," I said. "He was a man who worked hard all his life, Mr. Prager, and he came into a sum of money, you see, and he retired."

"Perhaps you could come to the point."

I took a silver dollar out of my pocket and gave it a spin, but, unlike Spinner, I kept my eyes on Prager's face instead of on the coin. He could have taken that face to any poker game in town and done just fine with it. Assuming he played his cards right.

"You don't see many of these," I said. "I went into a bank a couple of hours ago and tried to buy one. They just stared at me and then told me to go see a coin dealer. I thought a dollar was a dollar, you know? That's the way it used to be. It seems the silver content alone in these things is worth two or three bucks, and the collector value is even higher. I had to pay seven dollars for this thing, believe it or not."

"Why did you want it?"

"Just for luck. Mr. Jablon has a coin just like this one. Or at least it looked the same to me. I'm not a numismatist. That's a coin expert."

"I know what a numismatist is."

"Well, I only found that out today, while I was finding out that a dollar's not a dollar any more. Mr. Jablon could have saved me seven bucks if he'd left his dollar with me when he went out of town. But he left me something else that's probably worth a little more than seven dollars. See, he gave me this envelope full of papers and things. Some of them have your name on them. And your daughter's name, and some other names I mentioned. Michael Litvak, for example, but that's not a name you recognize, is it?"

The dollar had stopped spinning. Spinner had always snatched it up when it started to wobble, but I just let it drop. It landed heads.

"I thought since those papers had your name on them, along with those other names, I thought you might like to own them."

He didn't say anything, and I couldn't think of anything else to say. I picked up the silver dollar and gave it another spin. This time we both watched it. It stayed spinning for quite a while on the leather desk top. Then it glanced off a photograph in a silver frame, wobbled uncertainly, and landed heads again.

Prager picked up his desk phone and pushed a buzzer. He said, "That's all for today, Shari. Just put the machine on and go ahead home." Then, after a pause: "No, they can wait, I'll sign them tomorrow. You can head along home now. Fine."

Neither of us spoke until the door of the outer office opened and closed. Then Prager leaned back in his chair and folded his hands on his shirt front. He was a rather plump man, but there was no spare flesh on his hands. They were slender, with long fingers.

He said, "I gather you want to take up where—what was his name?"

"Jablon."

"Where Jablon took off."

"Something like that."

"I'm not a rich man, Mr. Scudder."

"You're not starving."

"No," he agreed. "I am not starving." He looked past me for a moment, probably at a seascape. He said, "My daughter Stacy went through a difficult period in her life. In the course of it, she had a very unfortunate accident."

"A little boy died."

"A little boy died. At the risk of sounding callous, I'll point out that that sort of thing happens all the time. Human beings—children, adults, what does it matter—people are killed accidentally every day."

I thought of Estrellita Rivera with a bullet in her eye. I don't know if anything showed in my face.

"Stacy's situation—her culpability, if you want to call if that—stemmed not from the accident but from her response after the fact. She didn't stop. If she had stopped, it would not have helped the boy at all. He was killed instantly."

"Did she know that?"

He closed his eyes for a moment. "I don't know," he said. "Is that pertinent?"

"Probably not."

"The accident . . . if she had stopped as she should have done, I'm sure she would have been exonerated. The boy rode his tricycle right off the curb in front of her."

"I understand she was on drugs at the time."

"If you want to call marijuana a drug."

"It doesn't matter what we call it, does it? Maybe she could have avoided the accident if she hadn't been stoned. Or maybe she would have had the judgment to stop once she hit the kid. Not that it matters any more. She was high, and she did hit the boy, and she didn't stop the car, and you managed to buy her off."

"Was I wrong to do that, Scudder?"

"How do I know?"

"Do you have children?" I hesitated, then nodded. "What would you have done?"

I thought about my sons. They weren't old enough to drive yet. Were they old enough to smoke marijuana? It was possible. And what would I do in Henry Prager's place?

"Whatever I had to do," I said. "To get them off."

"Of course. Any father would."

"It must have cost you a lot of money."

"More than I could afford. But I couldn't have afforded not to, you see."

I picked up my silver dollar and looked.at it. The date was 1878. It was a good deal older than I was, and had held up a lot better.

"I thought it was over," he said. "It was a nightmare, but I managed to straighten everything out. The people I dealt with, they realized that Stacy was not a criminal. She was a good girl from a good family who went through a difficult period in life. That's not uncommon, you know. They recognized that there was no reason to ruin a second life because a horrible accident had taken one life. And the experience—it's awful to say this, but it helped Stacy.

She grew as a result of it. She matured. She stopped using drugs, of course. And her life took on more purpose.''

''What's she doing now?''

''She's in graduate school at Columbia. Psychology. She plans to work with mentally retarded children.''

''She's what, twenty-one?''

''Twenty-two last month. She was nineteen at the time of the accident.''

''I suppose she has an apartment here in town?''

''That's correct. Why?''

''No reason. She turned out all right, then.''

''All my children turned out well, Scudder. Stacy had a difficult year or two, that's all.'' His eyes sharpened their focus suddenly. ''And how long do I have to pay for that one mistake? That's what I'd like to know.''

''I'm sure you would.''

''Well?''

''How deep did Jablon have the hook in you?''

''I don't understand.''

''What were you paying him?''

''I thought he was your associate.''

''It was a loose association. How much?''

He hesitated, then shrugged. ''The first time he came I gave him five thousand dollars. He gave the impression that one payment would be the end of it.''

''It never is.''

''So I understand. Then he came back a while later. He told me he needed more money. We finally put things on a business basis. So much a month.''

''How much?''

''Two thousand dollars a month.''

''You could afford that.''

"Not all that easily." He managed a small smile. "I was hoping I could find a way to deduct it, you know. Charge it to the business in some fashion."

"Did you find a way?"

"No. Why are you asking all this? Trying to determine just how much you can squeeze out of me?"

"No."

"This whole conversation," he said suddenly. "There's something wrong with it. You don't seem like a blackmailer."

"How so?"

"I don't know. That man was a weasel, he was calculating, slimy. You're calculating, but in a different way."

"It takes all kinds."

He stood up. "I won't go on paying indefinitely," he said. "I can't live with a sword hanging over me. Damn it, I shouldn't *have* to."

"We'll work something out."

"I don't want my daughter's life ruined. But I won't be bled to death."

I picked up the silver dollar and put it in my pocket. I couldn't make myself believe he had killed the Spinner, but at the same time I couldn't positively rule him out, and I was getting sick of the role I was playing. I pushed my chair back and got to my feet.

"Well?"

"I'll be in touch," I said.

"How much is it going to cost me?"

"I don't know."

"I'll pay you what I paid him. I won't pay any more than that."

"And how long will you pay me? Forever?"

"I don't understand."

"Maybe I can figure out something that'll make us

both happy,'' I said. 'I'll let you know when I do.''

"If you mean a single large payment, how could I trust you?''

"That's one of the things that has to be worked out,'' I said. "You'll hear from me.''

CHAPTER FIVE

I had arranged to meet Beverly Ethridge in the bar at the Hotel Pierre at seven o'clock. From Prager's office I walked to another bar, one on Madison Avenue. It turned out to be a hangout for advertising people, and the noise level was high and the tension unsettling. I had some bourbon and left.

On my way up Fifth Avenue, I stopped at St. Thomas's and slipped into a pew. I discovered churches not long after I left the force and moved away from Anita and the boys. I don't know what it is about them, exactly. They are about the only place in New York where a person has room to think, but I'm not sure that's their sole attraction for me. It seems logical to assume that there's some sort of personal quest involved, although I've no real idea what it might be. I don't pray. I don't think I believe in anything.

But they are perfect places to sit and think things out. I sat in St. Thomas's and thought about Henry Prager for a while. The thoughts didn't lead anywhere in particular. If he'd had a more expressive and less guarded face, I might have learned something one way or the other. He had done nothing to give himself away, but if he had been clever enough to nail the Spinner when the Spinner was already on guard, he'd be clever enough to give damned little away to me.

I had trouble seeing him as a murderer. At the same time, I had trouble seeing him as a blackmail victim. He didn't know it, and it was hardly time for me to tell him, but he should have told Spinner to take his dirt and shove it. So much money gets spread around to brush so many crimes under various rugs that no one really had anything resembling a hold on him. His daughter had committed a crime a couple of years ago. A really tough prosecutor might have gone for vehicular homicide, but more likely the charge would have been involuntary manslaughter and the sentence would have been suspended. Given those facts, there was really nothing much that could happen to her or to him this long after the fact. There might be a touch of scandal involved, but not enough to ruin either his business or his daughter's life.

So on the surface he had little motive for paying Spinner off, and less for killing him. Unless there was more to it than I knew about.

Three of them, Prager and Ethridge and Huysen-dahl, and they had all been paying silence money to Spinner until one of them decided to make the silence permanent. All I had to do was find out which was which.

And I really didn't want to.

For a couple of reasons. One of the best was that there was no way I could have as good a shot at the killer as the police could. All I had to do was dump Spinner's envelope on the desk of a good Homicide cop and let him play it out. The department's determination of time of death would be a lot more accurate than the vague estimate Koehler had given me. They could check alibis. They could put the three possibles through intensive interrogation, which all by itself would almost certainly be enough to open it all up.

There was just one thing wrong with that: The killer would wind up in slam, but the other two would come out with dirty faces. I came very close to passing it on to the cops anyway, figuring that none of the three had spotless faces to begin with. A hit-and-run killer, a hooker and con artist, a particularly nasty pervert—Spinner, with his personal code of ethics, had felt that he owed those innocent of his murder the silence they had purchased. But they had bought nothing from me, and I didn't owe them a thing.

The police would always be an option. If I never got a handle on things, they would remain as a last resort. But in the meantime I was going to make a try, and so I had made an appointment with Beverly Ethridge, I had dropped in on Henry Prager, and I would see Theordore Huysendahl sometime the next day. One way or another, they would all find out I was Spinner's heir and that the hook he'd had in them was in as deep as ever.

A group of tourists passed in the aisle, pointing out things to each other about the elaborate stone carvings above the high altar. I waited until they went by, sat for another minute or two, then got to my feet. On my way out I examined the offering boxes at the doors. You had your choice of furthering church work, overseas missions, or homeless children. I put three of Spinner's thirty hundred-dollar bills in the slot for homeless children.

There are certain things I do without knowing why. Tithing is one of them. A tenth of whatever I earn goes to whatever church I happen to visit after I've received the money. The Catholics get most of my business, not because I'm partial to them but because their churches are more apt to be open at odd times.

St. Thomas's is Episcopal. A plaque in front says they keep it open all week long so that passers-by will have a refuge from the turmoil of midtown Manhattan. I suppose the donations from tourists cover their overhead. Well, they now had a quick three hundred toward the light bill, courtesy of a dead blackmailer.

I went outside and headed uptown. It was time to let a lady know who was taking Spinner Jablon's place. Once they all knew, I would be able to take it easy. I could just sit back and relax, waiting for Spinner's killer to try killing me.

CHAPTER SIX

The cocktail lounge in the Pierre is illuminated by small candles set in deep blue bowls, one to a table. The tables are small and well separated from one another, round white tables with two or three blue velvet chairs at each. I stood blinking my eyes in the darkness and looking for a woman in a white pants suit. There were four or five unescorted women in the room, none of them wearing a pants suit. I looked instead for Beverly Ethridge, and found her at a table along the far wall. She was wearing a navy sheath and a string of pearls.

I gave my coat to the checkroom attendant and walked directly to her table. If she watched my approach, she did so out of the corner of her eye. Her head never turned in my direction. I sat down in the chair across from her, and only then did she meet my eyes. "I am expecting someone," she said, and her eyes slipped away, dismissing me.

"I'm Matthew Scudder," I said.

"Is that supposed to mean something to me?"

"You're pretty good," I said. "I like your white

pants suit, it becomes you. You wanted to see if I could recognize you so that you would know whether I had the pictures or not. I suppose that's clever, but why not just ask me to bring one along?''

Her eyes returned, and we took a few minutes to look at each other. It was the same face I'd seen in the pictures, but it was hard to believe it was the same woman. I don't know that she looked all that much older, but she did look a great deal more mature. More than that, there was an air of poise and sophistication that was quite incompatible with the girl in those pictures and on those arrest sheets. The face was aristocratic and the voice said good schools and good breeding.

Then she said, "A fucking cop," and her face and voice turned on the words and all the good breeding vanished. "How did you come up with it, anyway?"

I shrugged. I started to say something, but a waiter was on his way over. I ordered bourbon and a cup of coffee. She nodded at him to bring her another of what she was drinking. I don't know what it was. It had a lot of fruit in it.

When he was gone I said, "The Spinner had to leave town for a while. He wanted me to keep the business going in his absence."

"Sure."

"Sometimes things happen that way."

"Sure. You collared him and he threw me to you as his own ticket out. He had to get himself picked up by a crooked cop."

"Would you be better off with an honest one?"

She put one hand to her hair. It was straight and blonde, and styled in what I think they call a Sassoon cut. It had been considerably longer in the pictures, but the same color. Maybe the color was natural.

"An honest one? Where would I find one?"

"They tell me there's a couple around."

"Yeah, working traffic."

"Anyway, I'm not a cop. Just crooked." Her eyebrows went up. "I left the force a few years back."

"Then I don't get it. How do you wind up with the stuff?"

Either she was honestly puzzled or she knew Spinner was dead and she was very good indeed. That was the whole problem. I was playing poker with three strangers and I couldn't even get them all around the same table.

The waiter came around with the drinks. I sipped a little bourbon, drank a half inch of coffee, poured the rest of the bourbon into the cup. It's a great way to get drunk without getting tired.

"Okay," she said.

I looked at her.

"You'd better lay it out for me, Mr. Scudder." The well-bred voice now, and the face returning to its earlier planes. "I gather this is going to cost me something."

"A man has to eat, Mrs. Ethridge."

She smiled suddenly, whether spontaneously or not. Her whole face brightened with it. "I think you really ought to call me Beverly," she said. "It strikes me as odd to be addressed formally by a man who's seen me with a cock in my mouth. And what do they call you—Matt?"

"Generally."

"Put a price on it, Matt. What's it going to cost?"

"I'm not greedy."

"I bet you tell that to all the girls. How greedy aren't you?"

"I'll settle for the same arrangement you had with

Spinner. What's good enough for him is good enough for me."

She nodded thoughfully, a trace of a smile playing on her lips. She put the tip of one dainty finger to her mouth and gnawed it.

"Interesting."

"Oh?"

"The Spinner didn't tell you much. We didn't have an arrangement."

"Oh?"

"We were trying to work one out. I didn't want him to nickel me to death a week at a time. I did give him some money. I suppose it came to a total of five thousand dollars over the past six months."

"Not very much."

"I also went to bed with him. I would have preferred giving him more money and less sex, but I don't have much money of my own. My husband is a rich man, but that's not the same thing, you see, and I don't have very much money."

"But you've got a lot of sex."

She licked her lip in a very obvious way. That didn't make it any less provocative. "I didn't think you noticed," she said.

"I noticed."

"I'm glad."

I had some of my coffee. I looked around the room. Everybody was poised and well dressed, and I felt out of place. I was wearing my best suit, and I looked like a cop in his best suit. The woman across from me had made pornographic movies, prostituted herself, worked a confidence game. And she was completely at ease here, while I knew I looked out of place.

I said, "I think I'd rather have money, Mrs. Ethridge."

"Beverly."

"Beverly," I agreed.

"Or Bev, if you prefer. I'm very good, you know."

"I'm sure you are."

"I'm told I combine a professional's skill and an amateur's zeal."

"And I'm sure you do."

"After all, you've seen photographic proof."

"That's right. But I'm afraid I have a greater need for money than for sex."

She nodded slowly. "With Spinner," she said, "I was trying to arrange something. I don't have much cash available now. I sold some jewelry, things of that sort, but just to buy time. I could probably raise some money if I had a little time. I mean some substantial money."

"How substantial?"

She ignored the question. "Here's the problem. Look, I was on the game, you know that. It was temporary, it was what my psychiatrist calls a radical means of acting out inner anxieties and hostilities. I don't know what the fuck he's talking about, and I'm not sure he does either. I'm clean now, I'm a respectable woman, I'm a fucking jet-setter in a teensy way, but I know how the game works. Once you start paying, you wind up paying for the rest of your life."

"That's the usual pattern, all right."

"I don't want that pattern. I want to make one big buy and come up with everything. But it's hard to work out the mechanics of it."

"Because I could always have copies of the pictures."

"You could have copies. You could also just hold the information in your head, because the information is enough to wreck me."

"So you'd need a guarantee that one payment was all you'd ever have to make."

"That's right. I'd need to have a hook stuck in you so that you wouldn't even think about keeping any pictures. Or about coming back for another shot at me."

"It's a problem," I agreed. "You were trying to work it that way with Spinner?"

"That's right. Neither of us could come up with an idea that the other liked, and in the meantime I stalled him with sex and small change." She licked her lip. "It was rather interesting sex. His perceptions of me and all. I don't suppose a little man like that got much experience with young attractive women. And of course the social thing, the Park Avenue goddess, and at the same time he had those pictures and he knew things about me, so I became a special person for him. I didn't find him attractive. And I didn't like him, I didn't like his manner and I hated the hold he had over me. All the same, we did interesting things together. He was surprisingly inventive. I didn't like *having* to do things with him, but I liked *doing* them, if you know what I mean."

I didn't say anything.

"I could tell you some of the things we did."

"Don't bother."

"It might turn you on, listening."

"I don't think so."

"You don't like me much, do you?"

"Not too much, no. I can't really afford to like you, can I?"

She drank some of her drink, then licked her lips again. "You wouldn't be the first cop I ever took to bed," she said. "When you're in the game, that's a part of it. I don't think I ever met a cop who wasn't worried about his cock. That it was too small, that he wasn't good at using it. I suppose that's part of carrying a gun and a nightstick and all the rest of it, don't you think?"

"Could be."

"Personally, I always found cops to be built the same as anyone else."

"I think we're getting off the subject, Mrs. Ethridge."

"Bev."

"I think we ought to talk about money. One large sum of money, say, and then you can get off the hook and I can let go of the fishing rod."

"How much money are we talking about?"

"Fifty thousand dollars."

I don't know what sort of figure she was expecting. I don't know if she and Spinner had talked price while they rolled around on expensive sheets. She pursed her lips and gave a silent whistle, indicating that the sum I'd mentioned was a very large sum indeed.

She said, "You have expensive ideas."

"You pay it once and it's over."

"Back on Square A. How do I know that?"

"Because when you pay over the money, I give you a handle on me. I did something a few years ago. I could go to jail for it for a long time. I can write out a confession giving all the details. I'll give it to you when you pay the fifty thou, along with the stuff Spinner has on you. That locks me in, keeps me from doing a thing.''

''It wasn't just something like police corruption.''

''No, it wasn't.''

''You made somebody dead.''

I didn't say anything.

She took her time thinking it over. She took out a cigarette, tapped its end on a well-manicured nail. I guess she was waiting for me to light it for her. I remained in character and let her light it for herself.

Finally she said, ''It might work.''

''I'd be putting my neck in a noose. You wouldn't have to worry about me running out and yanking on the rope.''

She nodded. ''There's only one problem.''

''The money?''

''That's the problem. Couldn't we lower the price a little?''

''I don't think so.''

''I just don't have that kind of money.''

''Your husband does.''

''That doesn't put it in my handbag, Matt.''

''I could always eliminate the middleman,'' I said. ''Sell the goods directly to him. He'd pay.''

''You bastard.''

''Well? Wouldn't he?''

''I'll get the money somewhere. You bastard. He probably wouldn't pay, as a matter of fact, and then your hold's gone, isn't it? Your hold and my life, and we both wind up with nothing, and are you sure you want to risk that?''

''Not if I don't have to.''

''Meaning if I come up with the money. You've got to give me some time.''

"Two weeks."

She shook her head. "At least a month."

"That's longer than I planned on staying in town."

"If I can have it faster, I will. Believe me, the faster you're off my back the better I like it. But it might take me a month."

I told her a month would be all right but I hoped it wouldn't take that long. She told me I was a bastard and a son of a bitch, and then she turned abruptly seductive again and asked me if I wouldn't like to take her to bed anyway for the hell of it. I liked it better when she called me names.

She said, "I don't want you calling me. How can I get in touch with you?"

I gave her the name of my hotel. She tried not to show it, but it was obvious that my openness surprised her. Evidently the Spinner hadn't wanted her to know where she could find him.

I didn't blame him.

CHAPTER SEVEN

On his twenty-fifth birthday, Theodore Huysendahl had come into an inheritance of two and a half million dollars. A year later he'd added another million and change by marrying Helen Godwynn, and in the next five years or so he'd increased their total wealth to somewhere in the neighborhood of fifteen million dollars. At age thirty-two he sold his business interests, moved from a waterfront estate in Sands Point to a co-op apartment on Fifth Avenue in the Seventies, and devoted his life to public service. The President appointed him to a commission. The Mayor installed him as head of the Parks and Recreation Department. He gave good interviews and made good copy and the press loved him, and as a result he got his name in the papers a lot. For the past few years he'd been making speeches all over the state, turning up at every Democratic fund-raising dinner, calling press conferences all over the place, guesting occasionally on television talk shows. He always said that he was not running for governor, and I don't think even his own dog was dumb enough to buy that one. He was running, and running very hard, and he had a lot of money to spend and a lot of political favors to call, and he was tall and good-looking and radiantly charming, and if he had a political position, which was doubtful, it was not far enough to either the left or the right to alienate voters in the great middle.

The smart money gave him one shot in three at the nomination, and if he got that far he had a very strong chance for election. And he was only forty-one. He was probably already looking beyond Albany in the direction of Washington.

A handful of nasty little photographs could end all that in a minute.

He had an office in City Hall. I took the subway down to Chambers Street and headed over there, but first I detoured and walked up Center Street and stood in front of Police Headquarters for a few minutes. There was a bar across the street where we used to go before or after appearing in the Criminal Courts Building. It was a little early for a drink, though, and I didn't much want to run into anyone, so I went over to City Hall and managed to find Huysendahl's office.

His secretary was an older woman with wiry gray hair and sharp blue eyes. I told her I wanted to see him, and she asked my name.

I took out my silver dollar. "Watch closely," I said, and set it spinning on the corner of her desk. "Now just tell Mr. Huysendahl exactly what I've done, and that I'd like to see him in private. Now."

She scrutinized my face for a moment, probably in an attempt to assess my sanity. Then she reached for the telephone, but I put my hand gently atop hers.

"Ask him in person," I said.

Another long sharp look, with her head cocked

slightly to one side. Then, without quite shrugging, she got up and went into his office, closing the door after her.

She wasn't in there long. She came out looking puzzled and told me Mr. Huysendahl would see me. I'd already hung my coat on a metal rack. I opened Huysendahl's door, went in, closed it after me.

He started talking before he raised his eyes from the paper he was reading. He said, "I thought it was agreed that you were not to come here. I thought we established—"

Then he looked up and saw me, and something happened to his face.

He said, "You're not—"

I flipped the dollar into the air and caught it. "I'm not George Raft, either," I said. "Who were you expecting?"

He looked at me, and I tried to get something out of his face. He looked even better than his newspaper photos, and a lot better than the candid shots I had of him. He was sitting behind a gray steel desk in an office furnished with standard City-issue goods. He could have afforded to redecorate it himself—a lot of people in his position did that. I don't know what it said about him that he hadn't, or what it was supposed to say.

I said, "Is that today's *Times?* If you were expecting a different man with a silver dollar, you couldn't have read the paper very carefully. Third page of the second section, toward the bottom of the page."

"I don't understand what this is all about."

I pointed at the paper. "Go ahead. Third page, second section."

I stayed on my feet while he found the story and

read it. I'd seen it myself over breakfast, and I might have missed it if I hadn't been looking for it. I hadn't known whether it would make the paper or not, but there were three paragraphs identifying the corpse from the East River as Jacob "Spinner" Jablon and giving a few of the highlights of his career.

I watched carefully while Huysendahl read the squib. There was no way his reaction could have been anything other than legitimate. The color drained instantly from his face, and a pulse hammered in his temple. His hands clenched so violently that the paper tore. It certainly seemed to mean that he hadn't known Spinner was dead, but it could also mean he hadn't expected the body to come up and was suddenly realizing what a pot he was in.

"God," he said. "That's what I was afraid of. That's why I wanted—oh, *Christ!*"

He wasn't looking at me and he wasn't talking to me. I had the feeling that he didn't remember I was in the room with him. He was looking into the future and watching it go down the drain.

"Just what I was afraid of," he said again. "I kept telling him that. If anything happened to him, he said, a friend of his would know what to do with those . . . those pictures. But he had nothing to fear from me, I told him he had nothing to fear from me. I would have paid anything, and he knew that. But what would I do if he died? 'You better hope I live forever,' that's what he said." He looked up at me. "And now he's dead," he said. "Who *are* you?"

"Matthew Scudder."

"Are you from the police?"

"No. I left the department a few years ago."

He blinked. "I don't know . . . I don't know why you're here," he said. He sounded lost and helpless, and I wouldn't have been surprised if he had started to weep.

"I'm sort of a freelance," I explained. "I do favors for people, pick up the odd dollar here and there."

"You're a private detective?"

"Nothing that formal. I keep my eyes and ears open, that sort of thing."

"I see."

"Here I read this item about my old friend Spinner Jablon, and I thought it might put me in a position to do a favor for a person. A favor for you, as a matter of fact."

"Oh?"

"I figured that maybe Spinner had something that you'd like to have your hands on. Well, you know, keeping my eyes and ears open and all that, you never know what I might come up with. What I figured was that there might be some kind of a reward offered."

"I see," he said. He started to say something else, but the phone rang. He picked it up and started to tell the secretary that he wasn't taking any calls, but this one was from His Honor and he decided not to duck it. I pulled up a chair and sat there while Theodore Huysendahl talked with the Mayor of New York. I didn't really pay much attention to the conversation. When it ended, he used the intercom to stress that he was out to all callers for the time being. Then he turned to me and sighed heavily.

"You thought there might be a reward."

I nodded. "To justify my time and expenses."

"Are you the . . . friend Jablon spoke of?"

"I was a friend of his," I admitted.

"Do you have those pictures?"

"Let's say I might know where they are."

He rested his forehead on the heel of his hand and scratched his hair. The hair was a medium brown, not too long and not too short; like his political position, it was designed to avoid irritating anyone. He looked at me over the tops of his glasses and sighed again.

Levelly he said, "I would pay a substantial sum to have those pictures in hand."

"I can understand that."

"The reward would be . . . a generous one."

"I thought it probably would be."

"I can afford a generous reward, Mr. . . . I don't think I got your name."

"Matthew Scudder."

"Of course. I'm usually quite good at names, actually." His eyes narrowed. "As I said, Mr. Scudder, I can afford a generous reward. What I cannot afford is for that material to remain in existance." He drew a breath and straightened up in his chair. "I am going to be the next governor of the State of New York."

"So a lot of people say."

"More people will say it. I have scope, I have imagination, I have vision. I'm not a party hack in debt to the bosses. I'm independently wealthy, I'm not looking to enrich myself out of the public till. I could be an excellent governor. The state needs leadership. I could—"

"Maybe I'll vote for you."

He smiled ruefully. "I don't suppose it's time for a political speech, is it? Especially at a time when I'm so careful to deny that I'm a candidate. But you must see the importance of this to me, Mr. Scudder."

I didn't say anything.

"Did you have a specific reward in mind?"

"You'd have to set that figure. Of course, the higher it is, the more of an incentive it would be."

He put his fingertips together and thought it over. "One hundred thousand dollars."

"That's quite generous."

"That's what I would pay as a reward. For the return of absolutely everything."

"How would you know you got everything back?"

"I've thought of that. I had that problem with Jablon. Our negotiations were complicated by the difficulty I found in being in the same room with him. I knew instinctively that I would be at his mercy on a permanent basis. If I gave him substantial funds, he'd run through them sooner or later and be back for more money. Blackmailers always are, from what I understand."

"Usually."

"So I paid him so much a week. A weekly envelope, old bills out of sequence, as if I were paying ransom. As in a sense I was. I was ransoming all my tomorrows." He leaned back in his wooden swivel chair and closed his eyes. He had a good head, a strong face. I suppose there must have been weakness in it, because he had shown this weakness in his behavior, and sooner or later your character shows up in your face. It takes longer in some faces than in others; if there was weakness there, I couldn't spot it.

"All my tomorrows," he said. "I could afford that weekly payment. I could think of it"—that quick, rueful smile—"as a campaign expense. An ongoing one. What worried me was my continued vulnerability, not to Mr. Jablon but to what might come to pass should he die. My God, people die every day. Do you know how many New Yorkers are murdered in the average day?"

"It used to be three," I said. "A homicide once every eight hours, that was the average. I suppose it's higher now."

"The figure I heard was five."

"Higher in the summer. One week last July the tally ran over fifty. Fourteen of them in one day."

"Yes, I remember that week." He looked away for a moment, evidently lost in thought. I didn't know whether he was planning how to reduce homicide rates when he was governor or how to add my name to the list of victims. He said, "Can I assume that Jablon was murdered?"

"I don't see how you can assume anything else."

"I thought that might happen. I worried about it, that is. That sort of man, his kind runs a higher-than-average risk of being murdered. I'm sure I wasn't his only victim." His voice rose in pitch on the last words of the sentence, and he waited for me to confirm or deny his guess. I outwaited him, and he went on. "But even if he weren't murdered, Mr. Scudder, men die. They don't live forever. I didn't like paying that slimy gentleman every week, but the prospect of ceasing to pay him was significantly worse. He could die in any number of ways, anything at all. A drug overdose, say."

"I don't think he used anything."

"Well, you understand my point."

"He could have been hit by a bus," I said.

"Exactly." Another long sigh. "I can't go through this again. Let me state my case quite plainly. If you . . . recover the material. I'll pay you the figure I stated. One hundred thousand dollars, paid in any fashion you care to specify. Paid into a private Swiss account, if you prefer. Or handed over to you in cash. For that I'll expect the return of absolutely everything and your continued silence.''

"That makes sense.''

"I should think so.''

"But what guarantee would you have that you're getting what you pay for?''

His eyes studied me keenly before he spoke. "I think I'm rather good at judging men.''

"And you've decided I'm honest?''

"Hardly that. No insult intended, Mr. Scudder, but such a conclusion would be naive on my part, wouldn't it?''

"Probably.''

"What I have decided,'' he said, "is that you are intelligent. So let me spell things out. I will pay you the sum I've mentioned. And if, at any time in the future, you should attempt to extort further funds from me, on whatever pretext, I would make contact with . . . certain people. And have you killed.''

"Which might put you right on the spot.''

"It might,'' he agreed. "But in a certain position I would have to take just that chance. And I said before that I believe you are intelligent. What I meant was that I feel you would be intelligent enough to avoid finding out whether or not I'm bluffing. One hundred thousand dollars should be a sufficient reward. I don't think you'd be foolish enough to push your luck.''

I thought it over, gave a slow nod. "One question.''

"Ask it.''

"Why didn't you think of making this offer to the Spinner?''

"I did think of it.''

"But you didn't make it."

"No, Mr. Scudder, I did not."

"Why?"

"Because I didn't think he was sufficiently intelligent."

"I guess you were right about that."

"Why do you say that?"

"He wound up in the river," I said. "That wasn't very bright of him."

CHAPTER EIGHT

That was Thursday. I left Huysendahl's office a little before noon and tried to figure out what to do next. I'd seen all three of them now. They were all on notice, they all knew who I was and where to find me. I in turn had picked up a handful of facts about Spinner's operation and not very much more. Prager and Ethridge had given no indication of knowing the Spinner was dead. Huysendahl had seemed genuinely shocked and dismayed when I pointed it out to him. So far as I could tell, I'd accomplished nothing beyond making a target out of myself, and I wasn't even certain I'd done that right. It was conceivable I'd made myself all too reasonable a blackmailer. One of them had tried murder once, and it hadn't worked too well, so he might not be inclined to try it again. I could pick up fifty grand from Beverly Ethridge and twice that from Ted Huysendahl and some as yet undetermined sum from Henry Prager, and that would be just perfect except for one thing. I wasn't looking to get rich. I was looking to trap a killer.

The weekend floated on by. I spent a little time in

the microfilm room at the library, scanning old issues of the *Times* and picking up useless information on my three possibles and their various friends and relations. On the same page with an old story about a shopping center with which Henry Prager had been involved. I happened to see my own name. There was a story about a particularly good collar I had made about a year before I left the force. A partner and I had tagged a heroin wholesaler with enough pure smack to give the world an overdose. I would have enjoyed the story more if I hadn't known how it turned out. The dealer had a good lawyer, and the whole thing got thrown out on a technicality. The word at the time was that it had taken an even twenty-five thou to put the judge in the proper frame of mind.

You learn to get philosophical about things like that. We didn't manage to put the prick away, but we hurt him pretty good. Twenty-five for the judge, ten or fifteen easy for the lawyer, and on top of that he'd lost the smack, which left him out what he'd paid the importer plus what he could have expected to clear when he turned it over. I'd have been happier to see him in slam, but you take what you can get. Like the judge.

Sometime Sunday I called a number I didn't have to look up. Anita answered, and I told her a money order was on its way to her. "I came up with a couple of bucks," I said.

"Well, we can find a use for it," she said. "Thanks. Do you want to talk to the boys?"

I did and I didn't. They're getting to an age where it's a little easier for me to talk to them, but it's still awkward over the phone. We talked about basketball.

Right after I hung up, I had an odd thought. It occurred to me that I might not be talking to them again. Spinner had been a careful man by nature, a man who had made himself inconspicuous reflexively, a man who had felt most comfortable in deep shadows, and he still had not been careful enough. I was accustomed to open spaces, and in fact had to stay enough in the open to invite a murder attempt. If Spinner's killer decided to take a shot at me, he just might make it work.

I wanted to call back and talk to them again. It seemed that there ought to be something important for me to say, just on the off chance that I'd taken on more than I could carry. But I couldn't manage to think what it might be, and a few minutes later the impulse went away.

I had a lot to drink that night. It was just as well no one took a crack at me then. I'd have been easy.

Monday morning I called Prager. I'd left him on a very loose leash, and I had to give it a yank. His secretary told me he was busy on another line and asked if I would hold. I held for a minute or two. Then she came back to establish that I was still hanging in there, and then she put me through to him.

I said, "I've decided how we'll work this so that you're covered. There's something the police tried to hang on me that they could never make stick." He didn't know I'd been a cop myself. "I can write out a confession, include enough evidence to make it airtight. I'll give that to you as part of our deal."

It was basically the arrangement I'd tried out on Beverly Ethridge, and it made the same kind of sense to him that it had to her. Neither of them had managed to spot the joker in it, either: All I had to do was confess at great length to a crime that had never happened, and while my confession might make interesting reading, it would hardly enable anyone to hold a gun to my head. But Prager didn't figure out that part of it, so he liked the idea.

What he didn't like was the price I set.

"That's impossible," he said.

"It's easier than paying it in bits and pieces. You were paying Jablon two thousand a month. You'll pay me sixty in one chunk, that's less than three years' worth, and it'll all be over once and for all."

"I can't raise that kind of money."

"You'll find a way, Prager."

"I can't manage it."

"Don't be silly," I said. "You're an important man in your field, a success. If you don't have it in cash, you certainly have assets you can borrow against."

"I can't do it." His voice almost broke. "I've had . . . financial difficulties. Some investments haven't turned out to be what they should have been. The economy, there's less building, the interest rates are going crazy, just last week somebody raised the prime rate to ten percent—"

"I don't want an economics lesson, Mr. Prager. I want sixty thousand dollars."

"I've borrowed every cent I could." He paused for a moment. "I can't, I have no source—"

"I'll need the money fairly soon," I cut in. "I don't want to stay in New York any longer than I have to."

"I don't—"

"You do some creative thinking," I said. "I'll be in touch with you."

I hung up and sat in the phone booth for a minute

or two, until someone waiting to use it gave an impatient knock on the door. I opened the door and stood up. The man who wanted to use the phone looked as though he was going to say something, but he looked at me and changed his mind.

I wasn't enjoying myself. I was putting Prager through a wringer. If he'd killed Spinner, then maybe he had it coming. But if he hadn't, I was torturing him to no purpose, and the thought did not set well with me.

But one thing had come out of the conversation: He was hurting for money. And if Spinner, too, had been pushing for the fast final settlement, the big bite so that he could get out of town before someone killed him, that might have been enough to put the last bit of pressure on Henry Prager.

I'd been on the verge of ruling him out when I saw him in his office. I just didn't see that he had enough of a motive, but now he seemed to have a pretty good one after all.

And I'd just given him another.

I called Huysendahl a little later. He was out, so I left my number, and he called around two.

"I know I wasn't supposed to call you," I said, "but I have some good news for you."

"Oh?"

"I'm in a position to claim my reward."

"You managed to turn up that material?"

"That's right."

"Very quick work," he said.

"Oh, just sound detective procedure and a little bit of luck."

"I see. It may take some time to, uh, assemble the reward."

"I don't have very much time, Mr. Huysendahl."

"You have to be reasonable about this, you know. The sum we discussed is substantial."

"I understand you have substantial assets."

"Yes, but hardly in cash. Not every politician has a friend in Florida with that kind of money in a wall safe." He chuckled over the line, and seemed disappointed when I didn't join in. "I'll need some time."

"How much time?"

"A month at the outside. Perhaps less than that."

The role was easy enough, since I kept getting to rehearse it. I said, "That's not soon enough."

"Really? Just how much of a hurry are you in?"

"A big one. I want to get out of town. The climate doesn't agree with me."

"Actually, it's been rather mild the past few days."

"That's just the trouble. It's too hot."

"Oh?"

"I keep thinking about what happened to our mutual friend, and I wouldn't want it to happen to me."

"He must have made someone unhappy."

"Yeah, well, I've made a few people unhappy myself, My Huysendahl, and what I want to do is get the hell out of here within the week."

"I don't see how that would be possible." He paused for a moment. "You could always go and come back for the reward when things have had a chance to cool down somewhat."

"I don't think I'd like to do it that way."

"That's rather an alarming statement, don't you think? The sort of venture we've discussed requires a certain amount of give-and-take. It has to be a cooperative venture."

"A month is just too long."

"I might be able to manage it in two weeks."

"You might have to," I said.

"That sounds disturbingly like a threat,"

"The thing is, you're not the only person furnishing a reward."

"I'm not surprised."

"Right. And if I have to leave town before I can collect the reward from you, well, you never know what might happen."

"Don't be foolish, Scudder."

"I don't want to be. I don't think either of us should be foolish." I took a breath. "Look, Mr. Huysendahl, I'm sure it's nothing we can't work out."

"I certainly hope you're right."

"How does two weeks sound to you?"

"Difficult."

"Can you manage it?"

"I can try. I *hope* I can manage it."

"So do I. You know how to reach me."

"Yes," he said. "I know how to reach you."

I hung the phone up and poured a drink. Just a small one. I drank half of it and nursed the rest of it. The phone rang. I tossed down the last of the bourbon and picked it up. I thought it would be Prager. It was Beverly Ethridge.

She said, "Matt, it's Bev. I hope I didn't wake you?"

"You didn't."

"Are you alone?"

"Yes. Why?"

"I'm lonesome."

I didn't say anything. I remembered sitting across

the table from her, making it obvious that she wasn't getting to me. The performance had evidently convinced her. But I knew better. The woman was good at getting to people.

"I hoped we could get together, Matt. There are things we ought to talk about."

"All right."

"Would you be free around seven this evening? I've appointments until then."

"Seven's fine."

"The same place?"

I remembered how I had felt in the Pierre. This time we would meet on my turf. But not Armstrong's; I didn't want to take her there.

"There's a place called Polly's Cage," I said. "Fifty-seventh between Eighth and Ninth, middle of the block, the downtown side."

"Polly's Cage? It sounds charming."

"It's better than it sounds."

"Then I'll see you there at seven. Fifty-seventh between Eighth and Ninth—that's very near your hotel, isn't it?"

"It's across the street."

"That's very convenient," she said.

"It's handy for me."

"It might be handy for both of us, Matt."

I went out and had a couple of drinks and something to eat. Around six I got back to my hotel. I checked with the desk, and Benny told me I'd had three calls and there had been no messages.

I wasn't in my room ten minutes before the phone rang. I picked it up, and a voice I didn't recognize said, "Scudder?"

"Who's this?"

"You ought to be very careful. You go off half-cocked and upset people."

"I don't think I know you."

"You don't want to know me. All you gotta know is it's a big river, plenty of room in it, you don't want to try and fill it up all by yourself."

"Who wrote that line for you, anyway?"

The phone clicked.

CHAPTER NINE

I got to Polly's a few minutes early. There were four men and two women drinking at the bar. Behind it, Chuck was laughing politely at something one of the women had said. On the jukebox Sinatra was asking them to send in the clowns.

The room is a small one, with the bar on the right side as you enter. A railing runs the length of the room, and on the left of it there is an area a few steps up that contains about a dozen tables. They were all unoccupied now. I walked to the break in the railing, climbed the steps, and took the table that was farthest from the door.

Polly's gets most of its play around five, when thirsty people leave their offices. The really thirsty ones stick around longer than the rest, but the place doesn't pick up much passer-by trade, and almost always closes fairly early. Chuck pours generous drinks, and the five-o'clock drinkers usually tap out early on. On Fridays the TGIF crowd shows a certain amount of perseverance, but other times they generally lock up by midnight, and they don't even bother opening up on Saturdays or Sundays. It's a bar in the neighborhood without being a neighborhood bar.

I ordered a double bourbon, and had put half of it away by the time she walked in. She hesitated in the doorway, not seeing me at first, and some conversations died as heads turned her way. She seemed unaware of the attention she was drawing, or too accustomed to it to take notice of it. She spotted me, came over, and sat opposite me. The bar conversations resumed once it was established that she wasn't up for grabs.

She slid her coat off her shoulders and onto the back of her chair. She was wearing a hot-pink sweater. It was a good color for her, and an excellent fit. She took a pack of cigarettes and a lighter from her handbag. This time she didn't wait for me to light her cigarette. She drew in a lot of smoke, blew it out in a thin column, and watched with evident interest as it ascended toward the ceiling.

When the waitress came over she ordered gin and tonic. "I'm rushing the season," she said. "It's really too cold out for summer drinks. But I'm such a warm person emotionally that I can carry it off, don't you think?"

"Whatever you say, Mrs. Ethridge."

"Why do you keep forgetting my first name? Blackmailers shouldn't be so formal with their victims. It's easy for me to call you Matt. Why can't you call me Beverly?"

I shrugged. I didn't really know the answer myself. It was hard to be sure what was my own reaction to her and what was a part of the role I was playing. I didn't call her Beverly largely because she wanted me to, but that was an answer that only led to another question.

Her drink came. She put out her cigarette, sipped

her gin and tonic. She breathed deeply, and her breasts rose and fell within the pink sweater.

"Matt?"

"What?"

"I've been trying to figure out a way to raise the money."

"Good."

"It's going to take me some time."

I played them all the same way, and they all came back with the same response. Everybody was rich and nobody could get a few dollars together. Maybe the country was in trouble, maybe the economy was as bad as everybody said it was.

"Matt?"

"I need the money right away."

"You son of a bitch, don't you think I'd like to get this over with as soon as possible? The only way I could get the money is from Kermit, and I can't tell him what I need it for." She lowered her eyes. "Anyway, he hasn't got it."

"I thought he had more money than God."

She shook her head. "Not yet. He has an income, and it's substantial, but he doesn't come into the principal until he's thirty-five."

"When does that happen?"

"In October. That's his birthday. The Ethridge money is all tied up in a trust that terminates when the youngest child turns thirty-five."

"He's the youngest?"

"That's right. He'll come into the money in October. That's in six months. I've decided, I've even mentioned it to him, that I'd like to have some money of my own. So that I won't be dependent upon him to the extent that I am now. That's the kind of request he can understand, and he's more or less agreed to it. So in October he'll give me money. I don't know how much, but it will certainly be more than fifty thousand dollars, and then I'll be able to work things out with you.''

"In October."

"Yes."

"You won't have money in your hands then, though. There'll be a lot of paperwork involved. October's six months from now, and it'll be another six months easy before you've got cash in hand.''

"Will it really take that long?"

"Easily. So we're not talking about six months, we're talking about a year, and that's too long. Even six months is too long. Hell, *one* month is too long, Mrs. Ethridge. I want to get out of this town.''

"Why?"

"I don't like the climate."

"But spring's here. These are New York's best months, Matt.''

"I still don't like it."

She closed her eyes, and I studied her face in repose. The lighting in the room was perfect for her, paired electric candles glowing against the red flecked wallpaper. At the bar, one of the men got to his feet, picked up some of the change in front of him, and headed for the door. On the way out he said something, and one of the women laughed loudly. Another man entered the bar. Somebody put money in the jukebox, and Lesley Gore said it was her party and she would cry if she wanted to.

"You've got to give me time," she said.

"I haven't got it to give."

"Why do you have to get out of New York? What are you afraid of, anyway?"

"The same thing the Spinner was afraid of."

She nodded thoughtfully. "He was very nervous toward the end," she said. "It made the bed part very interesting."

"It must have."

"I wasn't the only one on his string. He made that fairly obvious. Are you playing his whole string, Matt? Or just me?"

"It's a good question, Mrs. Ethridge."

"Yeah, I like it myself. Who killed him, Matt? One of his other customers?"

"You mean he's dead?"

"I read newspapers."

"Sure. Sometimes your picture's in them."

"Yeah, and wasn't that just my lucky day. Did you kill him, Matt?"

"Why would I do that?"

"So that you could take his nice little number away from him. I thought you shook him down. Then I read how they fished him out of the river. Did you kill him?"

"No. Did you?"

"Sure, with my little bow and arrow. Listen, wait a year for your money and I'll double it. A hundred thousand dollars. That's nice interest."

"I'd rather take the cash and invest it myself."

"I told you I can't get it."

"How about your family?"

"What about them? They don't have any money."

"I thought you had a rich daddy."

She winced, and covered it by lighting another cigarette. Both our drinks were empty. I motioned to the waitress, and she brought fresh ones. I asked if there was any coffee made. She said there wasn't but she'd make a pot if I wanted. She sounded as though she really hoped I wouldn't want her to. I told her not to bother.

Beverly Ethridge said, "I had a rich great-grandfather."

"Oh?"

"My own father followed in his father's footsteps. The gentle art of turning a million dollars into a shoestring. I grew up thinking the money would always be there. That's what made everything that happened in California so easy. I had a rich daddy and I never really had to worry about anything. He could always bail me out. Even the serious things weren't serious."

"Then what happened?"

"He killed himself."

"How?"

"Sat in the car in a closed garage with the motor running. What's the difference?"

"None, I guess. I always wonder how people do it, that's all. Doctors usually use guns, did you know that? They have access to the simplest, cleanest ways in the world, an O.D. of morphine, anything like that, and instead they generally blow their brains out and make a hell of a mess. Why did he kill himself?"

"Because the money was gone." She picked up her glass, but paused with it halfway to her mouth. "That was why I came back east. All of a sudden he was dead, and instead of money there were debts. There was enough insurance so that my mother can live decently. She sold the house, moved to an apartment. With that and Social Security, she gets along." She took a long drink now. "I don't want to talk about it."

"All right."

"If you took those pictures to Kermit, you wouldn't get anything. You'd just queer your own pitch. He wouldn't buy them, because he wouldn't care about my good name. He'd just care about his own, which would mean getting rid of me and finding a wife as bloodless as he is."

"Maybe."

"He's playing golf this week. A pro-am tournament, they have them the day before the regular tournaments. He gets a professional golfer for a partner, and if they finish in the money the pro gets a few dollars out of it. Ketmit gets the glory. It's his chief passion, golf."

"I thought you were."

"I'm nicely ornamental. And I can act like a lady. When I have to."

"When you have to."

"That's right. He's out of town now, getting ready for this tournament. So I can stay out as late as I want. I can do as I please."

"Handy for you."

She sighed. "I guess I can't use sex this time, can I?"

"I'm afraid not."

"It's a shame. I'm used to using it, I'm damned good at it. Hell. A hundred thousand dollars a year from now is a lot of money."

"It's also a bird in the bush."

"I wish to hell I had something to use on you. Sex doesn't work, and I don't have money. I have a couple of dollars in a savings account, my own money."

"How much?"

"About eight thousand. I haven't had the interest entered in a long time. You're supposed to take the book in once a year. Somehow I never got around to it. I could give you what I've got, a down payment."

"All right."

"A week from today?"

"What's wrong with tomorrow?"

"Uh-uh." She shook her head emphatically. "No. All I can buy for my eight thousand is time, right? So I'm going to buy a week with it right off. A week from today you'll have the money."

"I don't even know you've got it."

"No, you don't."

I thought it over. "All right," I said finally. "Eight thousand dollars a week from today. But I'm not going to wait a year for the rest of it."

"Maybe I could turn some tricks," she said. "Like four hundred and twenty of 'em at a hundred dollars a throw."

"Or forty-two hundred at ten."

"You fucker," she said.

"Eight thousand. A week from today."

"You'll get it."

I offered to put her in a cab. She said she'd get her own and that I could pay for the drinks this time. I stayed at the table for a few minutes after she left, then paid the check and went out. I crossed the street and asked Benny if there were any messages. There weren't, but a man had called and not left his name. I wondered if it was the man who had threatened to put me in the river.

I went over to Armstrong's and took my usual table. The place was crowded for a Monday. Most of the faces were familiar. I had bourbon and coffee, and the third time around I caught a glimpse of a face

that looked familiar in an unfamiliar way. On her
next circuit of the tables, I crooked a finger at Trina.
She came over to me with her eyebrows up, and the
expression accented the feline cast to her features.

"Don't turn around," I said. "At the bar in front,
right between Gordie and the guy in the denim
jacket."

"What about him?"

"Probably nothing. Not right away, but in a
couple of minutes, why don't you walk past him and
get a look at him?"

"And then what, Cap'n?"

"Then report back to Mission Control."

"Aye-aye, sir."

I kept my eyes facing toward the door but concentrated on what I could see of him at the periphery of
my vision, and it wasn't my imagination. He did keep
glancing my way. It was hard to gauge his height,
because he was sitting down, but he looked almost
tall enough to play basketball. He had an outdoor
face and modishly long sand-colored hair. I couldn't
make out his features very well—he was the length of
the room away from me—but I got an impression of
cool, competent toughness.

Trina drifted back with a drink I hadn't gotten
around to ordering. "Camouflage," she said, setting
it before me. "I have given him the old once-over.
What did he do?"

"Nothing that I know of. Have you seen him
before?"

"I don't think so. In fact, I'm sure I haven't,
because I would remember him."

"Why?"

"He tends to stand out in a crowd. You know who

he looks like? The Marlboro man.''

"From the commercials? Didn't they use more than one guy?''

"Sure. He looks like all of them. You know, high rawhide boots and a wide-brimmed hat and smelling of horseshit, and the tattoo on his hand. He's not wearing boots or a hat, and he doesn't have the tattoo, but it's the same image. Don't ask me if he smells of horseshit. I didn't get close enough to tell.''

"I wasn't going to ask.''

"What's the story?''

"I'm not sure there is one. I think I saw him a little while ago in Polly's.''

"Maybe he's making the rounds.''

"Uh-huh. Same rounds I'm making.''

"So?''

I shrugged. "Probably nothing. Thanks for the surveillance work, away.''

"Do I get a badge?''

"And a decoder ring.''

"Neat,'' she said.

I waited him out. He was definitely paying attention to me. I couldn't tell whether he knew I was taking an interest in him as well. I didn't want to look straight at him.

He could have tagged me from Polly's. I wasn't sure I'd seen him there, just felt I'd noticed him somewhere or other. If he'd picked me up at Polly's, then it wasn't hard to tie him to Beverly Ethridge; she could have set up the date in the first place in order to put a tag on me. But even if he had been at Polly's, that didn't prove anything; he could have picked me up earlier and tailed me there. I hadn't been making myself hard to find. Everybody knew where I lived, and I'd spent the whole day in the neighborhood.

It was probably around nine thirty when I noticed him, maybe closer to ten. It was almost eleven when he packed it in and left. I had decided he was going to leave before I did, and I would have sat there until Billie closed the place if necessary. It didn't take that long, and I hadn't thought it would. The Marlboro man didn't look like the sort who enjoyed biding his time in a Ninth Avenue gin mill, even as congenial a gin mill as Armstrong's. He was too active and western and outdoorsy, and by eleven o'clock he had mounted his horse and ridden off into the sunset.

A few minutes after he left, Trina came over and sat down across from me. She was still on duty, so I couldn't buy her a drink. "I have more to report," she said. "Billie has never seen him before. He hopes he never sees him again, he says, because he does not like to serve alcoholic beverages to men with eyes like that."

"Eyes like what?"

"He did not go into detail. You could probably ask him. What else? Oh, yes. He ordered beer. Two of them, in about as many hours. Wurzburger dark, if you care."

"Not awfully."

"He also said—"

"Shit."

"Billie rarely says 'shit.' He says 'fuck' a lot, but rarely 'shit,' and he didn't say it now. What's the matter?"

But I was up from the table and on my way to the bar. Billie ambled over, polishing a glass with a towel. He said, "You move fast for a big man, stranger."

"My mind moves slow. That customer you had—"

"The Marlboro man, Trina calls him."

"That's the one. I don't suppose you got around to washing his glass yet, did you?"

"Yes, as a matter of fact I did. This is it here, as best I recall." He held it up for my inspection. "See? Spotless."

"Shit."

"That's what Jimmie says when I *don't* wash them. What's the matter?"

"Well, unless the bastard was wearing gloves, I have just done something stupid."

"Gloves. Oh. Fingerprints?"

"Uh-huh."

"I thought that only worked on the tube."

"Not, when they come as a gift. Like on a beer glass. Shit. If he ever comes in again, which would be too much to hope for—"

"I pick up the glass with a towel and put it some place very safe."

"That's the idea."

"If you'd told me . . ."

"I know. I should have thought of it."

"All I was interested in was seeing the last of him. I don't like people like him anywhere, and especially in bars. He made two beers last an hour apiece, and that was just fine with me. I was not about to push drinks on him. The less he drank and the sooner he left, the happier he made me."

"Did he talk at all?"

"Just to order the beers."

"You catch any kind of an accent?"

"Didn't notice it at the time. Let me think." He closed his eyes for a few seconds. "No. Standard American nondescript. I usually notice voices, and I can't dredge up anything special about his. I can't

believe he's from New York, but what does that
prove?"

"Not too much. Trina said you didn't like his
eyes."

"I didn't like them at all."

"How so?"

"The feeling they gave me. It's hard to describe. I
couldn't even tell you what color they were, although
I think they were light rather than dark. But there
was something about them, they stopped at the surface."

"I'm not sure I know what you mean."

"There was no depth to them. They could have
been glass eyes, almost. Did you happen to watch
Watergate?"

"Some of it. Not much."

"One of those pricks, one of the ones with a German name—"

"They all had German names, didn't they?"

"No, but there were two of them. Not Haldeman.
The other one."

"Ehrlichman."

"That's the prick. Did you happen to see him? Did
you notice his eyes? No depth to them."

"A Marlboro man with eyes like Ehrlichman."

"This isn't connected with Watergate or anything,
is it, Matt?"

"Only in spirit."

I went back to my table and had a cup of coffee. I'd
have liked to sweeten it with bourbon, but I decided
it wasn't sensible. The Marlboro man didn't figure to
try to take me tonight. There were too many people
who could place him at the scene. This was simple

reconnaissance. If he was going to try anything on, it would be some other time.

That was the way it looked to me, but I wasn't sure enough by my reasoning to walk home with too much bourbon in my bloodstream. I was probably right, but I didn't want to risk being very wrong.

I took what I'd seen of the guy and pasted in Ehrlichman's eyes and Billie's general impression of him, and I tried to match up the picture with my three angels. I couldn't make anything work. He could be some construction roughneck off one of Prager's projects, he could be a healthy young stud Beverly Ethridge liked to have around, he could be pro talent Huysendahl had hired for the occasion. Fingerprints would have given me a make on him, but my mental reflexes had been too slow for me to take advantage of the opportunity. If I could find out who he was I could come up around him from behind, but now I had to let him make his play and meet him head on.

I guess it was about twelve thirty when I paid my tab and left. I eased the door open carefully, feeling a little foolish, and I scanned both sides of Ninth Avenue in both directions. I didn't see my Marlboro man, or anything else that looked at all menacing.

I started toward the corner of Fifty-seventh Street, and for the first time since it all started I had the feeling of being a target. I had set myself up this way quite deliberately, and it had certainly seemed like a good idea at the time, but ever since the Marlboro man had turned up things had become very different. It was real now, and that was what made all the difference.

''There was movement in a doorway ahead of me, and I was up on the balls of my feet before I recognized the old woman. She was in her usual spot in the doorway of the boutique called Sartor Resartus. She's always there when the weather's decent. She always asks for money. Most of the time I give her something.

She said, "Mister, if you could spare—" and I found some coins in my pocket and gave them to her. "God will bless you," she said.

I told her I hoped she was right. I walked on toward the corner, and it's a good thing it wasn't raining that night, because I heard her scream before I heard the car. She let out a shriek, and I spun around in time to see a car with its high beams on vault the curb at me.

CHAPTER TEN

I didn't have time to think it over. I guess my reflexes were good. At least they were good enough. I was off balance from spinning around when the woman screamed, but I didn't stop to get my balance. I just threw myself to the right. I landed on a shoulder and rolled up against the building.

It was barely enough. If a driver has the nerve, he can leave you no room at all. All he has to do is bounce his car off the side of the building. That can be rough on the car and rough on the building, but it's roughest of all on the person caught between the two. I thought he might do that, and then when he yanked the wheel at the last minute I thought he might do it accidentally, fishtailing the car's rear end and swatting me like a fly.

He didn't miss by much. I felt a rush of air as the car hurtled past me. Then I rolled over and watched him cut back off the sidewalk and onto the avenue. He snapped off a parking meter on his way, bounced when he hit the asphalt, then put the pedal on the floor and hit the corner just as the light turned red. He sailed right through the light, but then, so do half the cars in New York. I don't remember the last time I saw a cop ticket anybody for a moving violation. They just don't have the time.

"These crazy, crazy drivers!"

It was the old woman, standing beside me now, making *tsk* sounds.

"They just *drink* their whiskey," she said, "and they *smoke* their reefers, and then they go out for a *joy* ride. You could have been killed."

"Yes."

"And after all that, he didn't even stop to see if you were all right."

"He wasn't very considerate."

"People are not considerate any more."

I got to my feet and brushed myself off. I was shaking, and badly rattled. She said, "Mister, if you could spare . . . " and then her eyes clouded slightly and she frowned at some private puzzlement. "No," she said. "You just gave me money, didn't you? I'm very sorry. It's difficult to remember."

I reached for my wallet. "Now this is a ten-dollar bill," I said, pressing it into her hand. "You make sure you remember, all right? Make sure you get the right amount of change when you spend it. Do you understand?"

"Oh, dear," she said.

"Now you'd better go home and get some sleep. All right?"

"Oh, dear," she said. "Ten dollars. A ten-dollar bill. Oh, God bless you, sir."

"He just did," I said.

Isaiah was behind the desk when I got back to the hotel. He's a light-skinned West Indian with bright

blue eyes and kinky rust-colored hair. He has large
dark freckles on his cheeks and on the backs of his
hands. He likes the midnight-to-eight shift because
it's quiet and he can sit behind the desk working
double-acrostics, toking periodcially from a bottle of
cough syrup with codeine in it.

He does the puzzles with a nylon-tipped pen. I
asked him once if it wasn't more difficult that way.
"Otherwise there is no pride in it, Mr. Scudder,"
he'd said.

What he said now was that I'd had no calls. I went
upstairs and walked down the hall to my room. I
checked to see if there was any light coming from
under the door, and there wasn't, and I decided that
didn't prove anything. Then I looked for scratch
marks around the lock, and there weren't any, and I
decided that that didn't prove anything either,
because you could pick those hotel locks with dental
floss. Then I opened the door and found there was
nothing in the room but the furniture, which stood to
reason, and I turned on the light and closed and
locked the door and held my hands at arm's length
and watched the fingers tremble.

I made myself a stiff drink and then I made myself
drink it. For a moment or two my stomach picked up
the shakes from my hands and I didn't think the
whiskey was going to stay down, but it did. I wrote
some letters and numbers on a piece of paper and put
it in my wallet. I got out of my clothes and stood
under the shower to wash off a coating of sweat. The
worst sort of sweat, composed of equal parts of exer-
tion and animal fear.

I was toweling dry when the phone rang. I didn't
want to pick it up. I knew what I was going to hear.

"That was just a warning, Scudder."

"Bullshit. You were trying. You're just not good enough."

"When we try, we don't miss."

I told him to fuck off and hung up. I picked it up a few seconds later and told Isaiah no calls before nine, at which time I wanted a wake-up call.

Then I got into bed to see whether I could sleep.

I slept better than I'd expected. I woke up only twice during the night, and both times it was the same dream, and it would have bored a Freudian psychiatrist to tears. It was a very literal dream, no symbols to it at all. Pure reenactment, from the moment I left Armstrong's to the moment the car closed on me, except that in the dream the driver had the necessary skill and balls to go all the way, and just as I knew he was going to put me between the rock and the hard place, I woke up, with my hands in fists and my heart hammering.

I guess it's a protective mechanism, dreaming like that. Your unconscious mind takes the things you can't handle and plays with them while you sleep until some of the sharp corners are worn off. I don't know how much good those dreams did, but when I awoke for the third and last time a half-hour before I was supposed to get my wake-up call, I felt a little better about things. It seemed to me that I had a lot to feel good about. Someone had tried for me, and that's what I had been looking to provoke all along. And someone had missed, and that was also as I wanted it.

I thought about the phone call. It had not been the Marlboro man. I was reasonably certain of that. The voice I'd heard was older, probably around my own age, and it had had the flavor of New York streets in its tones.

So there looked to be at least two of them in on it. That didn't tell me much, but it was something else to know, another fact to file and forget. Had there been more than one person in the car? I tried to remember what I had seen in the brief glimpse I'd had while the car was bearing down on me. I hadn't seen much, not with the headlights pitched right at my eyes. And by the time I'd turned for a look at the departing car, it was already a good distance past me and moving fast. And I'd been more intent on catching the plate number than counting heads.

I went downstairs for breakfast, but couldn't manage more than a cup of coffee and a piece of toast. I bought a pack of cigarettes out of the machine and smoked three of them with my coffee. They were the first I'd had in almost two months, and I couldn't have gotten a better hit if I'd punched them right into a vein. They made me dizzy but in a nice way. After I'd finished the three, I left the pack on the table and went outside.

I went down to Centre Street and found my way to the Auto Squad room. A pink-cheeked kid who looked to be fresh out of John Jay asked if he could help me. There were half a dozen cops in the room, and I didn't recognize any of them. I asked if Ray Landauer was around.

"Retired a few months ago," he said. To one of the others he called, "Hey, Jerry, when did Ray retire anyway?"

"Musta been October."

He turned to me. "Ray retired in October," he said. "Can I help you?"

"It was personal," I said.

"I can find his address if you want to give me a minute."

I told him it wasn't important. It surprised me that Ray had packed it in. He didn't seem old enough to retire. But he was older than me, come to think of it, and I had had fifteen years on the force and had been off it for more than five, so that made me retirement age myself.

Maybe the kid would have given me a peek at the hot-car sheet. But I would have had to tell him who I was and go through a lot of bullshit that wouldn't be necessary with someone I knew. So I left the building and started walking toward the subway. When an empty cab came along, I changed my mind and grabbed it. I told the driver I wanted the Sixth Precinct.

He didn't know where it was. A few years ago, if you wanted to drive a cab you had to be able to name the nearest hospital or police station or firehouse from any point in the city. I don't know when they dropped the test, but now all you have to do is be alive.

I told him it was on West Tenth, and he got there without too much trouble. I found Eddie Koehler in his office. He was reading something in the *News*, and it wasn't making him happy.

"Fucking Special Prosecutor," he said. "What's a guy like this accomplish except aggravate people?"

"He gets his name in the papers a lot."

"Yeah. Figure he wants to be governor?"

I thought of Huysendahl. "Everybody wants to be governor."

"That's the fucking truth. Why do you figure that is?"

"You're asking the wrong person, Eddie. I can't figure out why anybody wants to be anything."

His cool eyes appraised me. "Shit, you always wanted to be a cop."

"Since I was a kid. I never wanted to be anything else, as far back as I can remember."

"I was the same way. Always wanted to carry a badge. I wonder why. Sometimes I think it was how we were brought up, the cop on the corner, everybody respecting him. And the movies we saw as a kid. The cops were the good guys."

"I don't know. They always shot Cagney in the last reel."

"Yeah, but the fucker had it coming. You'd watch and you'd be crazy about Cagney but you wanted him to buy the farm at the end. He couldn't fucking get away with it. Sit down, Matt. I don't see you much lately. You want some coffee?"

I shook my head but I sat down. He took a dead cigar from his ashtray and put a match to it. I took two tens and a five from my wallet and put them on his desk.

"I just earned a hat?"

"You will in a minute."

"Just so the Special Prosecutor don't get wind of it."

"You don't have anything to worry about, do you?"

"Who knows? You get a maniac like that and everybody's got something to worry about." He folded the bills and put them in his shirt pocket. "What can I do for you?"

I got out the slip of paper I'd written on before going to bed. "I've got part of a license number," I said.

"Don't you know anybody at Twenty-sixth Street?"

That was where the Motor Vehicle people had their offices. I said, "I do, but it's a Jersey plate. I'm guessing the car was stolen and that you can turn it up on the G.T.A. sheet. The three letters are either LKJ or LJK. I only got a piece of the three numbers. There's a nine and a four, possibly a nine and two fours, but I don't even know the order."

"That should be plenty, if it's on the sheet. All this towing, sometimes people don't report thefts. They just assume we towed it, and they don't go down to the pound if they don't happen to have the fifty bucks, and then it turns out it was stolen. Or by then the thief dumped it and we *did* tow it away, and they wind up paying for a tow, but not from where they parked it. Hang on, I'll get the sheet."

He left his cigar in the ashtray, and it was out again by the time he got back. "Grand Theft Auto," he said. "Give me those letters again."

"LKJ or LJK."

"Uh-huh. You got a make and model on it?"

"Nineteen forty-nine Kaiser-Frazer."

"Huh?"

"Late-model sedan, dark. That's about as much as I got. They all look about the same."

"Yeah. Nothing on the main sheet. Let's see what came in last night. Oh, hello, LJK nine one four."

"That sounds like it."

"Seventy-two Impala two-door, dark green."

"I didn't count the doors, but that's got to be it."

"Belongs to a Mrs. William Raiken from Upper Montclair. She a friend of yours?"

"I don't think so. When did she report it?"

"Let's see. Two in the morning, it says here."

I had left Armstrong's around twelve thirty, so Mrs. Raiken hadn't missed her car right away. They could have put it back and she never would have known it was gone.

"Where did it come from, Eddie?"

"Upper Montclair, I suppose."

"I mean where did she have it parked when they swiped it?"

"Oh." He had closed the list; now he flipped it open to the last page. "Broadway and a Hundred Fourteenth. Hey, that leads to an interesting question."

It damn well did, but how did he know that? I asked him what question it led to.

"What was Mrs. Raiken doing on Upper Broadway at two in the morning? And did Mr. Raiken know about it?"

"You've got a dirty mind."

"I shoulda been a Special Prosecutor. What's Mrs. Raiken got to do with your missing husband?"

I looked blank, then remembered the case I'd invented to explain my interest in Spinner's corpse. "Oh," I said. "Nothing. I wound up telling his wife to forget it. I got a couple days' work out of it."

"Uh-huh. Who took the car and what did they do with it last night?"

"Destroyed public property."

"Huh?"

"They knocked over a parking meter on Ninth Avenue, then got the hell away in a hurry."

"And you just happened to be there, and so you just happened to catch the license number, and naturally you figured the car was stolen but you wanted to check because you're a public-spirited citizen."

"That's close."

"It's crap. Sit down, Matt. What are you into that I oughta know about?"

"Nothing."

"How does a stolen car tie into Spinner Jablon?"

"Spinner? Oh, the guy they took out of the river. No connection."

"Because you were just looking for this woman's husband." I saw my slip then, but waited to see if he'd caught it, and he had. "It was his girlfriend looking for him last time I heard it. You're being awful cute with me, Matt."

I didn't say anything. He picked his cigar out of the ashtray and studied it, then leaned over and dropped it in his wastebasket. He straightened up and looked at me, then away, then at me again.

"What are you holding out?

"Nothing you have to know."

"How do you get tied into Spinner Jablon?"

"It's not important."

"And what's with the car?"

"That's not important either." I straightened up. "Spinner got dropped in the East River, and the car sheared off a parking meter on Ninth between Fifty-seventh and Fifty-eighth. And the car was stolen uptown, so none of this has been going on in the Sixth Precinct. There's nothing you've got to know, Eddie."

"Who killed Spinner?"

"I don't know."

"Is that straight?"

"Of course it's straight."

"Are you playing tag with somebody?"

"Not exactly."

"Jesus Christ, Matt."

I wanted to get out of there. I wasn't holding out anything he had a claim on, and I really couldn't give him or anybody else what I had. But I was playing a lone hand and ducking his questions, and I could hardly expect him to like it.

"Who's your client, Matt?"

Spinner was my client, but I could see no profit in saying so. "I don't have one," I said.

"Then what's your angle?"

"I'm not sure I have an angle, either."

"I hear things to the effect that Spinner was in the dollars lately."

"He was well dressed the last time I saw him."

"That so?"

"His suit set him back three hundred and twenty dollars. He happened to mention it."

He looked at me until I averted my own gaze. In a low voice he said, "Matt, you don't want people driving cars at you. It's unhealthy. You sure you don't want to lay it all out for me?"

"As soon as it's time, Eddie."

"And you're sure it's not time yet?"

I took my time answering. I remembered the feel of that car rolling at me, remembered what actually happened, and then remembered how I dreamed it, with the driver taking the big car all the way to the wall.

"I'm sure," I said.

At the Lion's Head I had a hamburger and some bourbon and coffee. I was a little surprised that the car had been stolen so far uptown. They could have picked it up early on and parked it in my neighborhood, or the Marlboro man could have made a phone call between the time I left Polly's and the time he found his way into Armstrong's. Which would mean there were at least two people in the thing, which I had already decided on the basis of the voice

I'd heard over the telephone. Or he could have—

No, it was pointless. There were too many possible scenarios I could write for myself, and none of them was going to get me anywhere but confused.

I signaled for another cup of coffee and another shot, mixed them together, and worked on it. The tail end of my conversation with Eddie had gotten in the way. There was something I had learned from him, but the problem was that I didn't know that I knew it. He had said something that had rung a very muted bell, and I couldn't get it to ring again.

I got a dollar's worth of change and went over to the phone. Jersey Information gave me William Raiken's number in Upper Montclair. I called it and told Mrs. Raiken I was from the Auto Theft Squad, and she said was surprised we had recovered her car so soon and did I happen to know if it was at all damaged.

I said, "I'm afraid we haven't recovered your car yet, Mrs. Raiken."

"Oh."

"I just wanted to get some details. Your car was parked at Broadway and One Hundred Fourteenth Street?"

"That's right. On One Hundred Fourteenth, not on Broadway."

"I see. Now, our records indicate that you reported the theft at approximately two A.M. Was that immediately after you noticed the car was missing.

"Yes. Well, just about. I went to where I parked the car and it wasn't there, of course, and my first thought was it was towed away. I was parked legally, but sometimes there are signs you don't see, different regulations, but anyway they don't do any towing that far uptown, do they?"

"Not above Eighty-sixth Street."

"That's what I thought, although I always manage to find a legal space. Then I thought maybe I'd made a mistake and I actually left the car on a Hundred Thirteenth, so I went and checked, but of course it wasn't there either, so then I called my husband to have him pick me up, and he said to report the theft, so that was when I called you. Maybe there was fifteen or twenty minutes between when I missed the car and when I actually placed the call."

"I see." I was sorry now that I'd asked. "And when did you park the car, Mrs. Raiken?"

"Let me see. I had the two classes, an eight-o'clock short-story workshop and a ten-o'clock course in Renaissance history, but I was a little early, so I guess I parked a little after seven. Is that important?"

"Well, it won't aid in recovering the vehicle, Mrs. Raiken, but we try to develop data to pinpoint the times when various crimes are likely to occur."

"That's interesting," she said. "What good does that do?"

I had always wondered that myself. I told her it was part of the overall crime picture, which is what I generally had been told when I'd asked similar questions. I thanked her and assured her that her car would probably be recovered shortly, and she thanked me, and we said good-bye to each other and I went back to the bar.

I tried to determine what I'd learned from her and decided I'd learned nothing. My mind wandered, and I found myself wondering just what Mrs. Raiken had been doing on the Upper West Side in the middle of the night. She hadn't been with her husband, and her last class must have let out around eleven. Maybe she'd just had a few beers at the West End or one of the other bars around Columbia. Quite a few beers, maybe, which would explain why she'd walked around the block looking for her car. Not that it mattered if she'd had enough beer to float a battleship, because Mrs. Raiken didn't have a whole hell of a lot to do with Spinner Jablon or anybody else, and whether or not she had anything to do with Mr. Raiken was their business and none of my own, and—

Columbia.

Columbia is at One Hundred Sixteenth and Broadway, so that's where she would have been taking courses. And someone else was studying at Columbia, taking graduate courses in psychology and planning to work with retarded children.

I checked the phone book. No Prager, Stacy, because single women know better than to put their first names in telephone books. But there was a Prager, S., on West One Hundred Twelfth between Broadway and Riverside.

I went back and finished my coffee. I left a bill on the bar. At the doorway I changed my mind, looked up Prager, S., again, and made a note of the address and phone number. On the chance that S. stood for Seymour or anything other than Stacy, I dropped a dime in the slot and dialed the number. I let it ring seven times, then hung up and retrieved my dime. There were two other dimes with it.

Some days you get lucky.

CHAPTER ELEVEN

By the time I got off the subway at Broadway and One Hundred Tenth, I was a lot less impressed by the coincidence I had turned up. If Prager had decided to kill me, either directly or through hirelings, there was no particular reason why he would have stolen a car two blocks away from his daughter's apartment. It looked at first glance as though it ought to add up to something, but I wasn't sure that it did.

Of course, if Stacy Prager had a boyfriend, and if he turned out to be the Marlboro man . . .

It looked to be worth a try. I found her building, a five-story brownstone which now held four apartments to a floor. I rang her bell, and there was no answer. I rang a couple of other bells on the top floor—it's surprising how often people buzz you in that way—but no one was home, and the vestibule lock looked very easy. I used a pick on it, and I couldn't have opened it much faster with a key. I climbed three steep flights of stairs and knocked on the door of 4-C. I waited and knocked again, and then I opened both the locks on her door and made myself at home.

There was one fairly large room with a convertible

sofa and a sprinkling of Salvation Army furniture. I
checked the closet and the dresser, and all I learned
was that if Stacy had a boyfriend he lived elsewhere.
There was no signs of male occupancy.

I gave the place a very casual toss, just trying to get
some sense of the person who lived there. There were
a lot of books, most of them paperbacks, most of
them dealing with some aspect of psychology. There
was a stack of magazines: *New York* and *Psychology
Today* and *Intellectual Digest*. There was nothing
stronger than aspirin in the medicine chest. Stacy
kept her apartment in good order, and it in turn gave
the impression that her life was also in good order. I
felt a violator standing there in her apartment, scanning the titles of her books, rummaging through the
clothes in her closet. I grew increasingly uncomfort-
able in the role, and my failure to find anything to
justify my presence augmented the feeling. I got out
of there and closed up after myself. I locked one of
the locks; the other had to be locked with a key, and I
figured she would simply decide she had failed to
lock it on the way out.

I could have found a nice framed photo of the
Marlboro man. That would have been handy, but it
just hadn't happened. I left the building and went
around the corner and had a cup of coffee at a lunch
counter. Prager and Ethridge and Huysendahl, and
one of them had killed Spinner and had tried to kill
me, and I didn't seem to be getting anywhere.

Suppose it was Prager. Things seemed to form a
pattern, and although they didn't really lock in place,
they had the right sort of feel to them. He was on the
hook in the first place because of a hit-and-run case,
and so far a car had been used twice. Spinner's letter
mentioned a car jumping a curb at him, and one had
certainly taken a shot at me last night. And he was

the one who seemed to be feeling the bite financially. Beverly Ethridge was stalling for time, Theodore Huysendahl had agreed to my price, and Prager said he didn't know how he could raise the money.

So suppose it was him. If so, he had just tried to commit murder, and he hadn't made it work, and he was probably a little shaky about it. If it was him, now was a good time to rattle the bars of his cage. And if it wasn't him, I'd be in a better position to know it if I dropped in on him.

I paid for my coffee and went out and flagged a cab.

The black girl looked up at me when I entered his office. It took her a second or two to place me, and then her dark eyes took on a wary expression.

"Matthew Scudder," I said.

"For Mr. Prager?"

"That's right."

"Is he expecting you, Mr. Scudder?"

"I think he'll want to see me, Shari."

She seemed startled that I remembered her name. She got hesitantly to her feet and stepped out from behind the U-shaped desk.

"I'll tell him you're here," she said.

"You do that."

She slipped through Prager's door, drawing it swiftly shut behind her. I sat on the vinyl couch and looked at Mrs. Prager's seascape. I decided that the men were vomiting over the sides of the boat. There was no question about it.

The door opened and she returned to the reception room, again closing the door after her. "He'll see you in about five minutes," she said.

"All right."

"I guess you got important business with him."

"Fairly important."

"I just hope things go right. That man has not been himself lately. It just seems the harder a man works and the more successful he grows, that's all the more pressure he has bearing down upon him."

"I guess he's been under a lot of pressure lately."

"He has been under a strain," she said. Her eyes challenged me, holding me responsible for Prager's difficulty. It was a charge I could not deny.

"Maybe things will clear up soon," I suggested.

"I truly hope so."

"I suppose he's a good man to work for?"

"A very good man. He has always been—"

But she didn't get to finish the sentence, because just then there was the sound of a truck backfiring, except trucks do that at ground level, not on the twenty-second floor. She had been standing beside her desk, and she stayed frozen there for a moment, eyes wide, the back of her hand pressed to her mouth. She held the pose long enough for me to get out of my chair and beat her to his door.

I yanked it open, and Henry Prager was seated at his desk, and of course it had not been a truck backfiring. It had been a gun. A small gun, .22 or .25 caliber from the look of it, but when you put the barrel in your mouth and tilt it up toward the brain, a small gun is all you really need.

I stood in the doorway, trying to block it, and she was at my shoulder, small hands hammering at my back. For a moment I didn't yield, and then it seemed to me that she had at least as much right as I to look at him. I took a step into the room and she followed me and saw what she'd known she was going to see.

Then she started to scream.

CHAPTER TWELVE

If Shari hadn't known my name, I might have left. Perhaps not; cop instincts die hard if they die at all, and I had spent too many years despising those reluctant witnesses who slipped off into the shadows to feel comfortable playing the role myself. Nor would it have sat well to duck out on a girl in her condition.

But the impulse was surely present. I looked at Henry Prager, his body slumped over his desk, his features contorted in death, and I knew that I was looking at a man I had killed. His finger had pulled the trigger, but I'd put the gun in his hand by playing my game a little too well.

I had not asked to have his life intertwined with mine, nor had I sought to be a factor in his death. Now his corpse confronted me; one hand was stretched across the desk, as if pointing at me.

He had bribed his daughter's way out of an unintentional homicide. The bribery had laid him open to blackmail, which had provoked another homicide, this one intentional. And that first murder had only sunk the barb deeper—he was still being blackmailed, and he could always be tagged for Spinner's murder.

And so he had tried to murder again, and had failed. And I turned up in his office the next day, and so he told his secretary he wanted five minutes, but he'd taken only two or three of them.

He'd had the gun at hand. Perhaps he'd checked it earlier in the day to make sure it was loaded. And perhaps, while I waited in the outer office, he entertained thoughts of greeting me with a bullet.

But it is one thing to run a man down on a dark street at night or to knock a man unconscious and throw him in the river. And it is something else again to shoot a man in your own office with your secretary a few yards away. Perhaps he had measured out these considerations in his mind. Perhaps he had already resolved on suicide. I couldn't ask him now, and what did it matter? Suicide protected his daughter, while murder would have exposed everything. Suicide got him off a treadmill that turned faster than his legs could travel.

I had some of these thoughts as I stood there regarding his corpse, others in the hours that followed. I don't know how long I looked at him while Shari sobbed against my shoulder. Not all that long, I suppose. Then reflexes took over, and I steered the girl back to the outer office and made her sit on the couch. I picked up her phone and dialed 911.

The crew that caught it were from the Seventeenth Precinct over on East Fifty-first. The two detectives were Jim Heaney and a younger man named Finch— I didn't catch his first name. I had known Jim enough to nod to, and that made it a little easier, but even with total strangers I didn't look to be in for much trouble. Everything added up to suicide to begin with, and the girl and I could both confirm that Prager was all alone when the gun went off.

The lab boys went through the motions all the same, although their hearts weren't in it. They took a lot of pictures and made a lot of chalk marks, wrapped and bagged the gun, and finally zipped Prager into a body bag and got him out of there. Heaney and Finch took Shari's statement first so that she could go home and collapse on her own time. All they really wanted was for her to plug the standard gaps so that the coroner's inquest could return a verdict of suicide, so they fed her questions and confirmed that her boss had been depressed and edgy lately, that he had been evidently worried about business, that his moods had been abnormal and out of character, and, on the mechanical side, that she had seen him a few minutes before the shot sounded, that she and I had been sitting in the outer office at the time, and that we had entered simultaneously to find him dead in his chair.

Heaney told her that was fine. Someone would be around for a formal statement in the morning, and in the meantime Detective Finch would see her home. She said that wasn't necessary, she'd get a cab, but Finch insisted.

Heaney watched the two of them leave. "You bet Finch'll take her home," he said. "That's quite an ass on that little lady."

"I didn't notice."

"You're getting old. Finch noticed. He likes the black ones, especially built like that. Myself, I don't fool around, but I got to admit I get a kick out of working with Finch. If he gets half the ass he tells me about, he's gonna fuck himself to death. Tell you the truth, I don't think he makes any of it up, either. The

broads go for him." He lit a cigarette and offered the
pack to me. I passed. He said, "That girl now, Shari,
I'll give you odds he nails her."

"Not today he won't. She's pretty shaky."

"Hell, that's the best time. I don't know what the
hell it is, but that's when they want it the most. Go
tell a woman her husband got killed, like breaking
the news, now would you make a pass at a time like
that? Whatever she looks like, would you do it?
Neither would I. You should hear the stories that son
of a bitch tells. Couple of months ago we had this
ironworker falls off a girder, Finch has to break the
news to the wife. He tells her, she cracks up, he gives
her a hug to comfort her, pets her a little, and the
next thing he knows she's got his zipper down and
she's blowing him."

"That's if you take Finch's word for it."

"Well, if half what he says is true, and I think he's
straight about it. I mean, he tells me when he strikes
out, too."

I didn't much want to have this conversation, but
neither did I want to make my feelings obvious, so we
went through a few more stories of Finch's love life
and then wasted a few minutes reviewing mutual
friends. This might have taken longer had we known
each other better. Finally he picked up his clipboard
and concentrated on Prager. We went through the
automatic questions, and I confirmed what Shari had
told him.

Then he said, "Just for the record, any chance he
could've been dead before you got here?" When I
looked blank, he spelled it out. "This is off the wall,
but just for the record. Suppose she killed him, don't
ask me how or why, and then she waits for you or
somebody else to come in, and then she fakes talking

to him, and she's sitting with you, and she triggers a gun, I don't know, a thread or something, and then the two of you discover the body together and she's covered.''

"You better cut out all that television, Jim. It's affecting your brain.''

"Well, it *could* happen that way.''

"Sure. I heard him talking to her when she went inside. Of course, she could have set up a tape recorder—''

"All right, for Christ's sake.''

"If you want to explore all the possibilities—''

"I said it was just off the wall. You watch what they do on *Mission Impossible* and you wonder how criminals are so stupid in real life. So what the hell, a crook can watch television too, and maybe he picks up an idea. But you heard him talking, and we can forget tape recorders, and that settles that.''

Actually, I hadn't heard Prager talking, but it was a lot simpler to say that I had. Heaney wanted to explore possibilities; all I wanted to do was get out of there.

"How do you fit into this, Matt? You working for him?''

I shook my head. "Checking out some references.''

"Checking on Prager?''

"No. On somebody who used him for a reference, and my client wanted a fairly intensive check. I saw Prager last week and I was in the neighborhood so I dropped in to clear up a couple of points.''

"Who's the subject of the investigation?''

"What's the difference? Somebody who worked with him eight or ten years ago. Nothing to do with him knocking himself off.''

"You didn't really know him, then. Prager."

"Met him twice. Once, come to think of it, since I didn't really get to see much of him today. And I talked briefly with him on the phone."

"He in some kind of trouble?"

"Not any more. I can't tell you much, Jim. I didn't know the guy or much about his situation. He seemed depressed and agitated. As a matter of fact, he impressed me as thinking the world was after him. He was very suspicious the first time I saw him, as if I was part of a plot to harm him."

"Paranoia."

"Like that, yes."

"Yeah, it all fits together. Business troubles and the feeling everything's closing in on you, and maybe he thought you were going to hassle him today, or maybe he reached a point, you know, he's had it up to here and he just can't stand to see one more person. So he takes the gun out of the drawer and there's a bullet in his brain before he has time to think it over. I wish to God they'd keep those handguns off the market. They truck 'em in by the ton out of the Carolinas. What do you bet that was an unregistered gun?"

"No bet."

"He probably thought he was buying it for protection. Little rinky-dink Spanish gun, you could hit a mugger six times in the chest and not stop him, and all it's good for is blowing your brains out. Had a guy about a year ago, it wasn't even good for that. Decided to kill himself and only did half the job and he's a vegetable now. Now he *oughta* kill himself, the life he's got left to him, but he can't even move his hands." He lit another cigarette. "You want to drop around tomorrow and dictate a statement?"

I told him I could do better than that. I used Shari's typewriter and knocked out a short statement with all the facts in the right places. He read it over and nodded. "You know the form," he said. "Saves us all some time."

I signed what I'd typed up, and he added it to the papers on his clipboard. He shuffled through them and said, "His wife's where? Westchester. Thank Christ for that. I'll phone the cops up there and let them have the fun of telling her her husband's dead."

I caught myself just in time to keep from volunteering the information that Prager had a daughter in Manhattan. It wasn't something I was likely to know. We shook hands, and he said he wished Finch would get back. "The bastard scored again," he said. "He figured to. Just so he don't stick around for seconds. And he might. He really likes the spades."

"I'm sure he'll tell you all about it."

"He always does."

CHAPTER THIRTEEN

I went to a bar, but stayed only long enough to throw down two double shots, one right after the other. There was a time factor involved. Bars remain open until four in the morning, but most churches close up shop by six or seven. I walked over to Lexington and found a church I couldn't remember having been to before. I didn't notice the name of it. Our Lady of Perpetual Bingo, probably.

They were having some sort of service, but I didn't pay any attention to it. I lit a few candles and stuffed a couple of dollars in the slot, then took a seat in the rear and silently repeated three names over and over. Jacob Jablon, Henry Prager, Estrellita Rivera, three names, three candles for three corpses.

During the worst times after I shot and killed Estrellita Rivera, I had been unable to keep my mind from going over and over what had happened that night. I kept trying to repeal time and change the ending, like an antic projectionist reversing the film and drawing the bullet back into the barrel of the gun. In the new version that I wanted to superimpose on reality, all my shots were on target. There were no ricochets, or if there were they spent themselves harmlessly, or Estrellita spent an extra minute picking out peppermints in the candy store and wasn't in the wrong place at the wrong time, or—

There was a poem I'd had to read in high school, and it had nagged at me from somewhere in the back of my mind until one day I went to the library and ran it down. Four lines from Omar Khayyam:

> *The moving finger writes, and having writ*
> *Moves on. Nor all your piety and wit*
> *Can call it back to cancel half a line*
> *Nor all your tears wash out a word of it.*

I had tried hard to blame myself for Estrellita Rivera, but in a certain sense it wouldn't stick. I had been drinking, certainly, but not heavily, and my overall marksmanship that night could not be faulted. And it was proper for me to shoot at the robbers. They were armed, they were fleeing from one killing already, and there were no civilians in the line of fire. A bullet ricocheted. Those things happen.

Part of the reason I left the force was that those things happen and I did not want to be in a position where I could do wrong things for right reasons. Because I had decided that, while it might be true that the end does not justify the means, neither does the means justify the end.

And now I had deliberately programmed Henry Prager to kill himself.

I hadn't seen it that way, of course. But I couldn't see that it made too much difference. I had begun by pressuring him into attempting a second murder, something he would never have done otherwise. He had killed Spinner, but if I had simply destroyed

Spinner's envelope I'd have left Prager with no need ever to kill again. But I'd given him reason to try, and he had tried and failed, and then he'd been backed into a corner and chosen, impulsively or deliberately, to kill himself.

I could have destroyed that envelope. I had no contract with Spinner. I'd agreed only to open the envelope if I failed to hear from him. I could have given away the whole three thousand instead of a tenth of it. I had needed the money, but not that badly.

But Spinner had made a bet, and he'd turned out a winner. He had spelled it all out: "Why I think you'll follow through is something I noticed about you a long time ago, namely that you happen to think there is a difference between murder and other crimes. I am the same. I have done bad things all my life but never killed anybody and never would. I have known people who have killed which I've known for a fact or a rumor and would never get close to them. It is the way I am and I think that you are that way too . . ."

I could have done nothing, and then Henry Prager would not have wound up in a body bag. But there *is* a difference between murder and other crimes, and the world is a worse place for the murderers it allows to walk unpunished, as Henry Prager would have walked had I would have walked had I done nothing.

There should have been another way. Just as the bullet should not have ricocheted into a little girl's eye. And try telling all that to the moving finger.

Mass was still going on when I left. I walked a couple of blocks, not paying much attention to where I was, and then I stopped at a Blarney Stone and took communion.

• • •

It was a long night.

The bourbon kept refusing to do its job. I moved around a lot, because every bar I hit had one person in it whose company put me on edge. I kept seeing him in the mirror and taking him with me wherever I went. The activity and the nervous energy probably burned off a lot of the alcohol before it had a chance to get to me, and the time I spent walking around was time I could have more profitably spent sitting in one place and drinking.

The kind of bars I chose had something to do with keeping me relatively sober. I usually drink in dark quiet places where a shot is two ounces, three if they know you. Tonight I was hitting Blarney Stones and White Roses. The prices were considerably lower but the shot glasses were small, and when you paid for an ounce that's what you got, and even so it was apt to be about 30 percent water.

At one place on Broadway they had the basketball game on. I watched the last quarter on a big color set. The Knicks were down by a point when the quarter started, and wound up dropping it by twelve or thirteen. That was the fourth game for the Celtics.

The guy next to me said, "And next year they lose Lucas and DeBusschere, and Reed's knees are still gonna be shit, and Clyde can't do it all, so where the fuck are we?"

I nodded. What he said sounded reasonable to me.

"Even at the end of three, dead even for three periods, and they got Cowens and What's-his-name with five fouls, and then they can't find the basket. I mean, they don't fucking try, you know?"

"Must be my fault," I said.

"Huh?"

"They started falling apart when I started watching. It must be my fault."

He looked me over and backed off a step. He said, "Easy, guy. I didn't mean nothing."

But he'd read me wrong. I'd been absolutely serious.

I wound up at Armstrong's, where they pour perfectly fine drinks, but by then I'd lost my taste for it. I sat in the corner with a cup of coffee. It was a quiet night, and Trina had time to join me.

"I kept a weather eye open," she said, "but saw of him neither hide nor hair."

"How's that?"

"The cowboy. Just my cute little way of saying he hasn't been around tonight. Wasn't I supposed to keep watch, like a good Junior G-Man?"

"Oh, the Marlboro man. I thought *I* saw him tonight."

"Here?"

"No, earlier. I've been seeing a lot of shadows tonight."

"Is something wrong?"

"Yeah."

"Hey." She covered my hand with one of hers. "What's the matter, baby?"

"I keep finding new people to light candles for."

"I don't get you. You're not drunk, are you, Matt?"

"No, but not for lack of trying. I have had better days." I sipped coffee, put the cup down on the checkered cloth. I took out Spinner's silver dollar—correction, *my* dollar, I'd bought and paid for it—and I gave it a spin. I said, "Last night somebody tried to kill me."

"God! Around here?"

"A few doors down the block."

"No wonder you're—"

"No, that's not it. This afternoon I got even. I killed a man." I thought she would take her hand from atop mine, but she didn't. "I didn't exactly kill him. He stuck a gun in his mouth and pulled the trigger. A little Spanish gun, they truck them in by the ton from the Carolinas."

"Why do you say you killed him?"

"Because I put him in a room and the gun was the only door out of it. I boxed him in."

She looked at her watch. "Fuck it," she said. "I can leave early for a change. If Jimmie wants to sue me for half an hour, then the hell with him." She reached behind her neck with both hands to unfasten her apron. The movement emphasized the swell of her breasts.

She said, "Like to walk me home, Matt?"

We had used each other a few times over the months to keep the lonelies away. We liked each other in and out of bed, and both of us had the vital security of knowing it could never lead to anything.

"Matt?"

"I couldn't do you much good tonight, kid."

"You could keep me from getting mugged on the way home."

"You know what I mean."

"Yeah, Mr. Detective, but you don't know what *I* mean." She touched my cheek with her forefinger. "I wouldn't let you near me tonight anyway. You need a shave." Her face softened into a smile. "I was offering a little coffee and company," she said. "I think you could use it."

"Maybe I could."

"Plain old coffee and company."

"All right."

"Not tea and sympathy, nothing like that."

"Just coffee and company."

"Uh-huh. Now tell me it's the best offer you've had all day."

"It is," I said. "But that's not saying a hell of a lot."

She made good coffee, and she managed to come up with a pint of Harper's to flavor it with. By the time I was done talking, the pint had gone from mostly full to mostly empty.

I told her most of it. I left out anything that would make Ethridge or Huysendahl indentifiable, and I didn't spell out Henry Prager's smarmy little secret. I didn't mention his name, either, although she figured to dope it out for herself if she bothered to read the morning papers.

When I was finished she sat there for a few minutes, head tilted to one side, eyes half lidded, smoke drifting upward from her cigarette. At length she said she didn't see how I could have done things differently.

"Because suppose you managed to let him know that you weren't a blackmailer, Matt. Suppose you got a little more evidence together and went to him. You would have exposed him, wouldn't you?"

"One way or another."

"He killed himself because he was afraid of exposure, and that was while he thought you were a blackmailer. If he knew you were going to hand him over to the cops, wouldn't he have done the same thing?"

"He might not have had the chance."

"Well, maybe he was better off having the chance. Nobody forced him to take it, it was his decision."

I thought it over. "There's still something wrong."

"What?"

"I don't exactly know. Something doesn't fit together the way it should."

"You just have to have something to feel guilty about." I guess the line hit home enough to show in my face, because she blanched. "I'm sorry," she said. "Matt, I'm sorry."

"For what?"

"I was just, you know, being cute."

"Many a true word is et cetera." I stood up. "It'll look better in the morning. Things generally do."

"Don't leave."

"I had the coffee and company, and thanks for both. Now I'd better get on home."

She was shaking her head. "Stay over."

"I told you before, Trina—"

"I know you did. I don't particularly want to fuck either, as a matter of fact. But I really don't want to sleep alone."

"I don't know if I can sleep."

"Then hold me until I fall asleep, Please, baby?"

We went to bed together and held each other. Maybe the bourbon finally got around to working, or maybe I was more exhausted than I'd realized, but I fell asleep like that, holding her.

CHAPTER FOURTEEN

I woke up with my head throbbing and a liverish taste in the back of my throat. A note on her pillow advised me to help myself to breakfast. The only breakfast I could face was in the bottle of Harper's, and I helped myself to it, and, along with a couple of aspirins from her medicine cabinet and a cup of lousy coffee from the deli downstairs, it took some of the edge off the way I felt.

The weather was good and the air pollution lighter than usual. You could actually see the sky. I headed back to the hotel, picking up a paper on the way. It was almost noon. I don't usually get that much sleep.

I would have to call them, Beverly Ethridge and Theodore Huysendahl. I had to let them know that they were off the hook, that in fact they'd never actually been on it in the first place. I wondered what their reactions would be. Probably a combination of relief and some indignation about having been gulled. Well, that would be their problem. I had enough of my own.

I'd have to see them in person, obviously. I couldn't manage it over the phone. I didn't look for-

ward to it, but did look forward to having it behind
me. Two brief phone calls and two brief meetings
and I would never have to see either of them again.

I stopped at the desk. There was no mail for me,
but there was a phone message. Miss Stacy Prager
had called. There was a number where I was to call
her as soon as possible. It was the number I had
dialed from the Lion's Head.

In my room I checked through the *Times*. Prager
was on the obit page under a two-column headline.
Just his obituary, with the statement that he had died
of an apparently self-inflicted gunshot wound. It was
apparent, all right. I was not mentioned in the article.
I'd thought that was how his daughter might have
gotten my name. Then I looked at the message slip
again. She had called around nine the night before,
and the first edition of the *Times* wouldn't have hit
the street before eleven or twelve.

So that meant she'd learned my name from the
police. Or that she had heard it earlier, from her
father.

I picked up the phone, then put it down again. I
did not much want to talk to Stacy Prager. I couldn't
imagine that there was anything I wanted to hear
from her, and I knew there was nothing I wanted to
say to her. The fact that her father was a murderer
was not something she would learn from me, nor
would anyone else. Spinner Jablon had had the
revenge he'd purchased from me. So far as the rest of
the world was concerned, his case could remain in the
Open file forever. The police didn't care who had
killed him, and I didn't feel obliged to tell them.

I picked up the phone again and called Beverly
Ethridge. The line was busy. I broke the connection
and tried Huysendahl's office. He was out to lunch. I

waited a few minutes and tried the Ethridge number
again, and it was still busy. I stretched out on the bed
and closed my eyes, and the phone rang.

"Mr. Scudder? My name is Stacy Prager." A
young and earnest voice. "I'm sorry I haven't been
in. After I called last night I wound up taking the
train so I could be with my mother."

"I just got your message a few minutes ago."

"I see. Well, would it be possible for me to talk
with you? I'm at Grand Central, I could come to
your hotel or meet you wherever you say."

"I'm not sure how I could help you."

There was a pause. Then he said, "Maybe you
can't. I don't know. But you were the last person to
see my father alive, and I—"

"I didn't even see him yesterday, Miss Prager. I
was waiting to see him at the time it happened."

"Yes, that's right. But the thing is . . . listen, I'd
really like to meet with you, if that's all right."

"If there's anything I could help you with over the
telephone—"

"Couldn't I meet you?"

I asked her if she knew where my hotel was. She
said she did, and that she could be there in ten or
twenty minutes and she would phone me from the
lobby. I hung up and wondered how she had known
how to reach me. I'm not in the telephone book. And
I wondered if she'd known about Spinner Jablon,
and if she'd known about me. If the Marlboro man
was her boyfriend, and if she'd been in on the planning . . .

If so, it was logical to believe that she'd hold me
responsible for her father's death. I couldn't even
argue the point—I felt responsible myself. But I
couldn't really believe she'd have a cute little gun in

her handbag. I'd ragged Heaney about watching television. I don't watch all that much television myself.

It took her fifteen minutes, during which time I tried Beverly Ethridge again and got another busy signal. Then Stacy called from the lobby, and I went downstairs to meet her.

Long dark hair, straight, parted in the middle. A tall, slender girl with a long, narrow face and dark, bottomless eyes. She wore clean well-tailored blue jeans and a lime-green cardigan sweater over a simple white blouse. Her handbag had been made by cutting the legs off another pair of jeans. I decided it was highly unlikely there was a gun in it.

We confirmed that I was Matthew Scudder and she was Stacy Prager. I suggested coffee, and we went to the Red Flame and took a booth. After they gave us the coffee, I told her I was very sorry about her father but that I still couldn't imagine why she wanted to see me.

"I don't know why he killed himself," she said.

"Neither do I."

"Don't you?" Her eyes searched my face. I tried to imagine her as she had been a few years ago, smoking grass and dropping pills, running down a child and freaking out sufficiently to drive away from what she'd done. That image failed to jibe with the girl seated across the Formica table from me. She now seemed alert and aware and responsible, wounded by her father's death but strong enough to ride it out.

She said, "You're a detective."

"More or less."

"What does that mean?"

"I do some private work on a free-lance basis. None of it as interesting as it may sound."

"And you were working for my father?"

I shook my head. "I'd seen him once last week," I said, and went on to repeat the cover story I'd given Jim Heaney. "So I really didn't know your father at all."

"That's very strange," she said.

She stirred her coffee, added more sugar, stirred it again. She took a sip and put the cup back in the saucer. I asked her why it was strange.

She said, "I saw my father the night before last. He was waiting at my apartment when I got home from classes. He took me out for dinner. He does that—did that—once or twice a week. But usually he would call me first to arrange it. He said he just had the impulse and took the chance that I'd be coming home."

"I see."

"He was very upset. Is that the right word? He was agitated, he was unsettled about something. He was always inclined to be a moody man, very exuberant when things were going right, very depressed when they weren't. When I was first getting into Abnormal Psych and studied the manic-depressive syndrome I got tremendous echoes of my father. I don't mean that he was insane in any sense of the word, but that he had the same kind of mood swings. They didn't interfere with his life, it was just that he had that type of personality."

"And he was depressed the night before last?"

"It was more than depression. It was a combination of depression and the kind of hyperactive nervousness you can get on speed. I would have thought he had taken some amphetamines except I know how he feels about drugs. I had a period of drug use a few years ago and he made it pretty clear how he felt, so I didn't really believe he was on anything."

She drank some more coffee. No, there was no gun in her purse. This was a very open girl. If she had a gun she'd have used it immediately.

She said, "We had dinner in a Chinese restaurant in the neighborhood. That's the Upper West Side, that's where I live. He hardly touched his food. I was very hungry myself, but I kept picking up his vibrations and I wound up not eating very much either. His conversation kept rambling all over the place. He was very concerned about me. He asked several times if I ever used drugs any more. I don't, and I told him so. He asked about my classes, if I was happy with my coursework and if I felt I was on the right track so far as how I would be earning a living. He asked if I was involved with anybody romantically, and I said I wasn't, nothing serious. And then he asked me if I knew you."

"He did?"

"Yes. I said the only Scudder I knew was the Scudder Falls Bridge. He asked if I had ever been to your hotel—he named the hotel and asked if I had been there—and I said I hadn't. He said that was where you lived. I didn't really understand what he was driving at."

"Neither do I."

"He asked if I ever saw a man spin a silver dollar. He took a quarter and spun it on the top of the table and asked if I had ever seen a man do that with a silver dollar. I said no, and I asked him if he was feeling all right. He said he was fine, and that it was very important that I shouldn't worry about him. He said if anything happened to him that I would be all right and not to worry."

"Which made you more concerned than ever."

"Of course. I was afraid . . . I was afraid of all kinds of things, and scared even to think of them. Like I thought he might have been to the doctor and found out there was something wrong with him. But I called the doctor he always goes to, I did that last night, and he hadn't been there since his annual physical last November, and there was nothing wrong with him then except slightly high blood pressure. Of course, maybe he went to some other doctor, there's no way of knowing unless it shows up in the autopsy. They have to do an autopsy in cases like this. Mr. Scudder?"

I looked at her.

"When they called me, when I found out he had killed himself, I wasn't surprised."

"You expected it?"

"Not consciously. I didn't really expect it, but once I heard, it all seemed to fit. In some way or other, I guess I knew he was trying to tell me he was going to die, trying to tie off the ends before he did it. But I don't know why he did it. And then I heard that you were there when he did it, and I remembered his asking me about you, if I knew you, and I wondered how you fit into it all. I thought maybe there was some problem in his life and you were investigating it for him, because the policeman said you were a detective, and I wondered . . . I just don't understand what it was all about."

"I can't imagine why he mentioned my name."

"You really weren't working for him?"

"No, and I hadn't had very much contact with him, it was just a superficial matter of confirming another man's references."

"Then it doesn't make sense."

I considered. "We did talk for a while last week," I said. "I suppose it's possible something I said seemed to have a special impact on his thinking. I can't imagine what it might have been, but we had one of those rambling conversations, and he might have picked up on something without my noticing it."

"I suppose that would have to be the explanation."

"I can't conceive of anything else."

"And then, whatever it was, it stayed on his mind. So he brought up your name because he couldn't bring himself to mention what it was that you said, or what it meant to him. And then when his secretary said you were there it must have sort of triggered things in his mind. *Triggered*. That's an interesting choice of word, isn't it?"

It had triggered things, the girl's announcing my presence. There was no question about it.

"I can't make anything out of the silver dollar. Unless it's the song. 'You can spin a silver dollar on a barroom floor and it'll roll because it's round.' What's the next line? Something about a woman never knows what a good man she has until she loses him, something like that. Maybe he meant he was losing everything now, I don't know. I guess his mind, I guess it wasn't terribly clear at the end."

"He must have been under a strain."

"I guess so." She looked away for a moment. "Did he ever say anything to you about me?"

"No."

"Are you sure?"

I pretended to concentrate, then said I was sure.

"I just hope he realized that everything's all right with me now. That's all. If he had to die, if he thought he had to die, I at least hope he knew I'm okay."

"I'm sure he did."

She'd been going through a lot since they called her and told her. Longer than that: since that dinner at the Chinese place. And she was going through plenty now. But she wasn't going to cry. She wasn't a crier. She was a strong one. If he'd had half her strength, he wouldn't have had to kill himself. He would have told Spinner to go screw himself in the first place, and he wouldn't have paid blackmail money, wouldn't have killed once, wouldn't have had to try to kill a second time. She was stronger that he had been. I don't know how much pride you can take in that kind of strength. You either have it or you don't.

I said, "So that was the last time you saw him. At the Chinese restaurant."

"Well, he walked me back to my apartment. Then he drove home."

"What time was that? That he left your place."

"I don't know. Probably around ten or ten thirty, maybe a little later. Why do you ask?"

I shrugged. "No reason. Call it habit. I was a cop for a lot of years. When a cop runs out of things to say, he finds himself asking questions. It hardly matters what the questions are."

"That's interesting. A kind of a learned reflex."

"I suppose that's the term for it."

She drew a breath. "Well," she said. "I want to thank you for meeting with me. I wasted your time—"

"I have plenty of time. I don't mind wasting some of it now and then."

"I just wanted to learn whatever I could about . . . about him. I thought there might be something, that he would have had some last message for me. A note, or a letter he might have mailed. I guess it's part of not really believing he's dead, that I can't believe I'll never hear from him one way or the other. I thought—well, thank you, anyway."

I didn't want her to thank me. She had no reason on earth to thank me.

An hour or so later, I reached Beverly Ethridge. I told her I had to see her.

"I thought I had until Tuesday. Remember?"

"I want to see you tonight."

"Tonight's impossible. And I don't have the money yet, and you agreed to give me a week."

"It's something else."

"What?"

"Not over the phone."

"Jesus," she said. "Tonight is absolutely impossible, Matt. I have an engagement."

"I thought Kermit was out playing golf."

"That doesn't mean I sit home alone."

"I can believe that."

"You really are a bastard, aren't you? I was invited to a party. A perfectly respectable party, the kind where you keep your clothes on. I could meet you tomorrow if it's absolutely necessary."

"It is."

"Where and when?"

"How about Polly's? Say around eight o'clock."

"Polly's Cage. It's a little tacky, isn't it?"

"A little," I agreed.

"And so am I, huh?"

"I didn't say that."

"No, you're always the perfect gentleman. Eight o'clock at Polly's. I'll be there."

I could have told her to relax, that the ball game was over, instead of letting her spend another day under pressure. But I figured she could handle the pressure. And I wanted to see her face when I let her off the hook. I don't know why. Maybe it was the particular kind of spark we struck off each other, but I wanted to be there when she found out that she was home free.

"Huysendahl and I didn't strike those sparks. I tried him at his office and couldn't reach him, and on a hunch I tried him at home. He wasn't there, but I managed to talk to his wife. I left a message that I would be at his office at two the next afternoon and that I would call again in the morning to confirm the appointment.

"And one other thing," I said. "Please tell him that he has absolutely nothing to worry about. Tell him everything's all right now and everything will work out fine."

"And he'll know what that means?"

"He'll know," I said.

I napped for a while, had a late bite at the French place down the block, then went back to my room and read for a while. I came very close to making an early night of it, but around eleven my room started to feel a little bit more like a monastic cell than it generally does. I'd been reading *The Lives of the Saints*, which may have had something to do with it.

Outside it was trying to make up its mind to rain. The jury was still out. I went around the corner to

Armstrong's. Trina gave me a smile and brought me a drink.

I was only there for an hour or so. I did quite a bit of thinking about Stacy Prager, and even more about her father. I liked myself a little less now that I'd met the girl. On the other hand, I had to agree with what Trina had suggested the night before. He had indeed had the right to pick that way out of his trouble, and now at least his daughter was spared the knowledge that her father had killed a man. The fact of his death was horrible, but I could not easily construct a scenario which would have worked out better.

When I asked for the check Trina brought it over and perched on the edge of my table while I counted out bills. "You're looking a little cheerier," she said.

"Am I?"

"Little bit."

"Well, I had the best night's sleep I've had in a while."

"Is that so? So did I, strangely enough."

"Good."

"Quite a coincidence, wouldn't you say?"

"Hell of coincidence."

"Which proves there are better sleeping aids than Seconal."

"You've got to use them sparingly, though."

"Or you get hooked on them?"

"Something like that."

A guy two tables away was trying to get her attention. She gave him a look, then turned back to me. She said, "I don't think it'll ever get to be a habit. You're too old and I'm too young and you're too withdrawn and I'm too unstable and we're both generally weird."

"No argument."

"But once in a while can't hurt, can it?"

"No."

"It's even kinda nice."

I took her hand and gave it a squeeze. She grinned quickly, scooped up my money, and went off to find out what the pest two tables down wanted. I sat there watching her for a moment, then got up and went out the door.

It was raining now, a cold rain with a nasty wind behind it. The wind was blowing uptown and I was walking downtown, which didn't make me particularly happy. I hesitated, wondering if I ought to go back inside for one more drink and give it a chance for the worst of it to blow over. I decided it wasn't worth it.

So I started walking toward Fifty-seventh Street, and I saw the old beggarwoman in the doorway of Sartor Resartus. I didn't know whether to applaud her industry or worry about her; she wasn't usually out on nights like this. But it had been clear until recently, so I decided she must have taken her post and then found herself caught in the rain.

I kept walking, reaching into my pocket for change. I hoped she wouldn't be disappointed, but she couldn't expect ten dollars from me every night. Only when she saved my life.

I had the coins ready, and she came out of the doorway as I reached it. But it wasn't the old woman.

It was the Marlboro man, and he had a knife in his hand.

CHAPTER FIFTEEN

He came at me in a rush, the knife held underhand and arcing upward, and if it hadn't been raining he would have had me cold. But I got a break. He lost his footing on the wet pavement and had to check the knife thrust in order to regain his balance, and that gave me time to react enough to duck back from him and set myself for his next try.

I didn't have to wait long. I was up on the balls of my feet, arms loose at my sides, a tingling sensation in my hands and a pulse working in my temple. He rocked from side to side, his broad shoulders hinting and feinting, and then he came at me. I'd been watching his feet and I was ready. I dodged to the left, pivoted, threw a foot at his kneecap. And missed, but bounced back and squared off again before he could set himself for another lunge.

He began circling to his left, circling like a prize-fighter stalking an opponent, and when he'd completed a half circle and had his back to the street, I figured out why. He wanted to corner me so that I couldn't make a run for it.

He needn't have bothered. He was young and trim

and athletic and outdoorsy. I was too old and carried too much weight, and for too many years the only exercise I had got was bending my elbow. If I tried to run, all I'd manage to do would be to give him my back for a target.

He leaned forward and began transferring the knife from hand to hand. That looks good in the movies, but a really good man with a knife doesn't waste his time that way. Very few people are really ambidextrous. He had started off with the knife in his right hand, and I knew it would be in his right hand when he made his next pass, so all he did with his hand-to-hand routine was give me breathing space and let me tune in on his timing.

He also gave me a little hope. If he'd waste energy with games like that, he wasn't all that great with a knife, and if he was amateur enough I had a chance.

I said, "I don't have much money on me, but you're welcome to it."

"Don't want your money, Scudder. Just you."

Not a voice I'd heard before, and certainly not a New York voice. I wondered where Prager had found him. After having met Stacy, I was fairly sure he wasn't her type.

"You're making a mistake," I said.

"It's your mistake, man. And you already made it."

"Henry Prager killed himself yesterday."

"Yeah? I'll have to send him some flowers." Back and forth with the knife, knees tensing, relaxing. "I'm gonna cut you up pretty, man."

"I don't think so."

He laughed. I could see his eyes now by the light of the street lamps, and I knew what Billie meant. He had killer eyes, psychopath eyes.

I said, "I could take you if we both had knives."

"Sure you could, man."

"I could take you with an umbrella." And what I really wished I had was an umbrella or a walking stick. Anything that gives you a little reach is a better defense against a knife than another knife. Better than anything short of a gun.

I wouldn't have minded a gun just then, either. When I left the police department, one immediate benefit was that I no longer had to carry a gun every waking moment. It was very important to me at the time not to carry a gun. Even so, for months I'd felt naked without one. I had carried one for fifteen years, and you sort of get used to the weight.

If I'd had a gun now, I'd have had to use it. I could tell that about him. The sight of a gun wouldn't make him drop the knife. He was determined to kill me, and nothing would keep him from trying. Where had Prager found him? He wasn't professional talent, certainly. Lots of people hire amateur killers, of course, and unless Prager had some mob connections I didn't know about, he wouldn't be likely to have access to any of the pro hit men.

Unless—

That almost started me on a whole new train of thought, and the one thing I couldn't afford to do was let my mind wander. I came back to reality in a hurry when I saw his feet change their shuffling pattern, and I was ready when he closed in on me. I had my moves figured and I had him timed, and I started my kick just as he was getting into his thrust, and I was lucky enough to get his wrist. He lost his balance but managed not to take a spill, and while I managed to jar the knife loose from his hand, it didn't sail far enough to do me much good. He caught his balance and reached for the knife, and got it before my foot did. He scrambled backward almost to the edge of the curb, and before I could jump him he had the knife at his side and I had to back off.

"Now you're dead, man."

"You talk a good game. I almost had you that time."

"I think I'll cut you in the belly, man. Let you go out nice and slow."

The more I kept talking, the more time he'd take between rushes. And the more time he took, the better chance there was that someone would join the party before the guest of honor wound up on the end of the knife. Cabs cruised by periodically, but not many of them, and the weather had cut the pedestrian traffic down to nothing. A patrol car would have been welcome, but you know what they say about cops, they're never around when you want 'em.

He said, "Come on, Scudder. Try and take me."

"I've got all night."

He rubbed his thumb across the blade of the knife. "It's sharp," he said.

"I'll take your word for it."

"Oh, I'll prove it to you, man."

He backed off a little, moving in the same shuffling gait, and I knew what was coming. He was going to commit himself to one headlong rush, and that meant it wouldn't be a fencing match any more, because if he didn't stab me on the first lunge he'd wind up tumbling me to the ground and we'd wrestle around there until only one of us got up. I watched his feet and avoided getting taken in by the shoulder fakes, and when he came I was ready.

I dropped to one knee and went way down after he'd already committed himself, and his knife hand went over my shoulder and I came up under him, my arms around his legs, and in one motion I spun and heaved. I got my legs into it and threw him as high and as far as I could, knowing he'd drop the knife when he landed, knowing I'd be on him in time to kick it away and put a toe into the side of his head.

But he never did drop the knife. He went high into the air and his legs kicked at nothing and he turned lazily in midair like an Olympic diver, but when he came down there was no water in the swimming pool. He had one hand extended to break the fall, but he didn't land right. The impact of his head on the concrete was like that of a melon dropped from a third-floor window. I was fairly sure he'd have a skull fracture, and that can be enough to kill you.

I went over and looked at him and knew it didn't matter if his skull was fractured or not, because he had landed on the back of his head while falling forward, and he was now in a position you can't achieve unless your neck is broken. I looked for a pulse, not expecting to find one, and I couldn't get a beat. I rolled him over and put my ear to his chest and didn't hear anything. He still had the knife in his hand, but it wouldn't do him any good now.

"Holy shit."

I looked up. It was one of the neighborhood Greeks who did his drinking at Spiro and Antares. We would nod at each other now and then. I didn't know his name.

"I saw what happened," he said. "Bastard was tryin' to kill you."

"That's just what you can help me explain to the police."

"Shit, no. I didn't see nothin', you know what I mean?"

I said, "I don't care what you mean. How hard do you think it'll be for me to find you if I want to? Go back into Spiro's and pick up the phone and dial nine one one. You don't even need a dime to do it. Tell 'em you want to report a homicide in the Eighteenth Precinct and give 'em the address."

"I don't know about that."

"You don't have to know anything. All you have to do is what I just told you."

"Shit, there's a knife in his hand, anybody can see it was self-defense. He's dead, huh? You said homicide, and the way his neck's bent. Can't walk the fuckin' streets any more, the whole fuckin' city's a fuckin' jungle."

"Make the call."

"Look—"

"You dumb son of bitch, I'll give you more aggravation than you'd ever believe. You want cops driving you crazy for the rest of your life? Go make the call."

He went.

I kneeled down next to the body and gave it a fast but thorough frisk. What I wanted was a name, but there was nothing on him to identify him. No wallet, just a money clip in the shape of a dollar sign. Sterling silver, it looked like. He had a little over three hundred dollars. I put the ones and fives back into the clip and returned it to his pocket. I stuffed the rest into my own pocket. I had more of a use for it than he did.

Then I stood there waiting for the cops to show and wondering if my little friend had called them. While I was waiting, a couple of cabs stopped from

time to time to ask what had happened and if they
could help. Nobody'd taken the trouble while the
Marlboro man was waving the knife at me, but now
that he was dead everybody wanted to live danger-
ously. I shooed them all away and waited some more,
and finally a black-and-white turned at Fifty-seventh
Street and ignored the fact that Ninth Avenue runs
one way downtown. They cut the siren and trotted
over to where I was standing over the body. Two men
in plainclothes; I didn't recognize either of them.

I explained briefly who I was and what had happened. The fact that I was an ex-cop myself didn't
hurt a bit. Another car pulled up while I was talking,
with a lab crew, and then an ambulance.

To the lab crew I said, "I hope you're going to
print him. Not after you get him to the morgue. Take
a set of prints now."

They didn't ask who I was to be giving orders. I
guess they assumed I was a cop and that I probably
ranked them pretty well. The plainclothes guy I'd
been talking to raised his eyebrows at me.

"Prints?"

I nodded. "I want to know who he is, and he
wasn't carrying any I.D."

"You bothered to look?"

"I bothered to look."

"Not supposed to, you know."

"Yes, I know. But I wanted to know who would
take the trouble to kill me."

"Just a mugger, no?"

I shook my head. "He was following me around
the other day. And he was waiting for me tonight,
and he called me by name. Your average mugger
doesn't research his victims all that carefully."

"Well, they're printing him, so we'll see what we

come up with. Why would anybody want to kill you?''

I let the question go by. I said, ''I don't know if he's local or not. I'm sure somebody'll have a sheet on him, but he may never have taken a fall in New York.''

''Well, we'll take a look and see what we got. I don't think he's a virgin, do you?''

''Not likely.''

''Washington'll have him if we don't. Want to come over to the station? Probably a few of the boys you know from the old days.''

''Sure,'' I said. ''Gagliardi still making the coffee?''

His face clouded. ''He died,'' he said. ''Just about two years ago. Heart attack, he was just sitting at his desk and he bought it.''

''I never heard. That's a shame.''

''Yeah, he was all right. Made good coffee, too.''

CHAPTER SIXTEEN

My preliminary statement was sketchy. The man who took it, a detective named Birnbaum, noticed as much. I'd simply said that I had been assaulted by a person unknown to me at a specific place and time, that my assailant had been armed with a knife, that I had been unarmed, and that I had taken defensive measures which had involved throwing my assailant in such a way that, though I had not so intended, the ensuing fall had resulted in his death.

"This punk knew you by name," Birnbaum said. "That's what you said before."

"Right."

"That's not in here." He had a receding hairline, and he paused to rub where the hair had previously been. "You also told Lacey he'd been following you around past couple of days."

"I noticed him once I'm sure of, and I think I saw him a few other times."

"Uh-huh. And you want to hang around while we trace the prints and try to figure out who he was."

"Right."

"You didn't wait to see if we turned up any I.D.

on him. Which means you probably looked and saw he wasn't carrying anything.''

"Maybe it was just a hunch," I suggested. "Man goes out to murder somebody, he doesn't carry identification around. Just an assumption on my part.''

He raised his eyebrows for a minute, then shrugged. "We can let it go at that, Matt. Lot of times I check out an apartment when nobody's home, and wouldn't you know it that they got careless and left the door open, because of course I wouldn't think of letting myself in with a loid."

"Because that would be breaking-and-entering."

"And we wouldn't want that, would we?" He grinned, then picked up my statement again. "There's things you know about this bird that you don't want to tell. Right?"

"No. There's things I *don't* know."

"I don't get it."

I took one of his cigarettes from the pack on the desk. If I wasn't careful I'd get the habit again. I spent some time lighting up, getting the words in the right order.

I said, "You're going to be able to clear a case off the books, I think. A homicide."

"Give me a name."

"Not yet."

"Look, Matt—"

I drew on the cigarette. I said, "Let me do it my way for a little while. I'll fill in part of it for you, but nothing goes on paper for the time being. You've got enough already to wrap what happened tonight as justifiable homicide, don't you? You got a witness and you've got a corpse with a knife in his hand."

"So?"

"The corpse was hired to tag me. When I know

who he is I'm probably going to know who hired
him. I think he was also hired to kill somebody else a
while ago, and when I know his name and background I'll be able to come up with evidence that
should lock right into the person who's paying the
check."

"And you can't open up on any of this in the
meantime?"

"No."

"Any particular reason?"

"I don't want to get the wrong person in trouble."

"You play a very lone hand, don't you?"

I shrugged.

"They're checking downtown right now. If he
doesn't show there, we'll wire the prints down to the
Bureau in D.C. It could add up to a long night."

"I'll hang around, if it's all right."

"I'd just as soon you did, matter of fact. There's a
couch in the loot's office if you want to close your
eyes for a while."

I said I'd wait until the word came back from
downtown. He found something to do, and I went
into an empty office and picked up a newspaper. I
guess I fell asleep, because the next thing I knew,
Birnbaum was shaking my shoulder. I opened my
eyes.

"Nothing downtown, Matt. Our boy's never taken
a bust in New York."

"That's what I thought."

"I thought you didn't know anything about him."

"I don't. I'm running hunches, I told you that."

"You could save us trouble if you told us where to
look."

I shook my head. "I can't think of anything faster
than wiring Washington."

"His prints are already on the wire. Might be a couple of hours anyway, and it's getting light outside already. Why don't you go home, and I'll give you a call soon as anything comes in."

"You got a full set. Doesn't the Bureau do this sort of things by computer these days?"

"Sure. But somebody has to tell the computer what to do, and they tend to take their time down there. Go home and get some sleep."

"I'll wait."

"Suit yourself." He started for the door, then turned to remind me about the couch in the lieutenant's office. But the time I'd dozed in the chair had taken the edge off the urge to sleep. I was exhausted, certainly, but sleep was no longer possible. Too many mental wheels were starting to turn, and I couldn't shut them off.

He had to be Prager's boy. It just had to add up that way. Either he had somehow missed the news that Prager was dead and out of the picture, or he was tied in close to Prager and wanted me dead out of spite. Or he had been hired through an intermediary, somehow, and didn't know that Prager was a part of it. Something, anything, because otherwise—

I didn't want to think about the otherwise.

I had been telling Birnbaum the truth. I had a hunch, and the more I thought about it the more I believed in it, and at the same time I kept wanting to be wrong. So I sat around the station house and read newspapers and drank endless cups of weak coffee and tried not to think about all of the things I couldn't possibly avoid thinking about. Somewhere along the line Birnbaum went home, after he'd briefed another detective named Guzik, and around nine thirty Guzik came over to me and said they had a make from Washington.

He read it off the teletype sheet. "Lundgren, John Michael. Date of birth fourteen March 'forty-three. Place of birth San Bernardino, California. Whole trail of arrests here, Matt. Living off immoral earnings, assault, assault with a deadly weapon, grand theft auto, grand larceny. He did local bits all up and down the West Coast, pulled some hard time in Quentin."

"He pulled a one-to-five in Folsom," I said. "I don't know whether they called it extortion or larceny. That would have been fairly recent."

He looked up at me. "I thought you didn't know him."

"I don't. He was working a badger game. Arrested in San Diego, and his partner turned state's evidence and got off. Sentence suspended."

"That's more detail than I've got here."

I asked him if he had a cigarette. He said he didn't smoke. He turned to ask if anybody had a cigarette, but I told him to forget it. "Get somebody with a steno pad," I said. "There's a lot to tell."

I gave them everything I could think of. How Beverly Ethridge had worked her way in and out of the world of crime. How she had married well and turned herself back into the society type she had been in the first place. How Spinner Jablon had pieced it all together on the strength of a newspaper photo and turned it into a neat little blackmail operation.

"I guess she stalled him for a while," I said. "But it kept being expensive, and he kept pushing for bigger money. Then her old boyfriend Lundgren came east and showed her a way out. Why pay blackmail when it's so much easier to kill the blackmailer? Lundgren was a pro as a criminal but an amateur as a killer. He tried a couple of different methods on Spinner. Tried to get him with a car, then wound up hitting him over the head and putting him in the East River. Then he tried for me with the car.''

''And then with the knife.''

''That's right.''

''How did you get into it?''

I explained, leaving out the names of Spinner's other blackmail victims. They didn't like that much, but there wasn't anything much they could do about it. I told them how I had staked myself out as a target and how Lundgren had taken the bait.

Guzik kept interrupting to tell me I should have given everything to the cops right off, and I kept telling him it was something I had not been willing to do.

''We'd've handled it right, Matt. Jesus, you talk about Lundgren's an amateur, shit, you ran around like an amateur yourself and almost got your ass in the wringer. You wound up going up against a knife with nothing but your hands, and it's dumb luck you're alive this minute. The hell, you ought to know better, you were a cop fifteen years, and you act like you don't know what the department's all about.''

''How about the people who didn't kill Spinner? What happens to them if I hand you the whole thing right off the bat?''

''That's their lookout, isn't it? They come into it with dirty hands. They got something to hide, that shouldn't be getting in the way of a murder investigation.''

''But there was no investigation. Nobody gave a shit about Spinner.''

''Because you were withholding evidence.''

I shook my head. "That's horseshit," I said. "I
didn't have evidence that anybody killed Spinner. I
had evidence that he was blackmailing several people. That was evidence against Spinner, but he was
dead, and I didn't think you were particularly anx-
ious to take him out of the morgue and throw him in
a cell. The minute I had murder evidence I put it in
your hand. Look, we could argue all day. Why don't
you put out a pickup order on Beverly Ethridge?"

"And charge her with what?"

"Two counts of conspiracy to murder."

"You've got the blackmail evidence?"

"In a safe place. A safe-deposit box. I can bring it
here in an hour."

"I think I'll come along with you and get it."

I looked at him.

"Maybe I want to see just what's in the envelope,
Scudder."

It had been *Matt* up until then. I wondered what
kind of a number he wanted to run. Maybe he was
just fishing, but he had visions of something or
other. Maybe he wanted to take my place in the
blackmail dodge, only he'd want real money, not the
name of a murderer. Maybe he figured the other
pigeons had committed real crimes and he could buy
himself a commendation by knocking them off. I
didn't know him well enough to guess which motiva-
tion would be consistent with the man, but it didn't
really make very much difference.

"I don't get it," I said. "I give you a homicide
collar on a silver platter and you want to melt down
the platter."

"I'm sending a couple boys over to pick up
Ethridge. In the meantime, you and me are going to
open up a safe-deposit box."

"I could forget where I left the key."

"And I could make your life difficult."

"It's not that much of a cinch as it is. It's just a few blocks from here."

"Still raining," he said. "We'll take a car."

We drove over to the Manufacturers Hanover branch at Fifty-seventh and Eighth. He left the black-and-white in a bus stop. All that to save a three-block walk, and it wasn't raining all that hard any more. We went inside and went down the stairs to the vault, and I gave my key to the guard and signed the signature card.

"Had the damnedest thing you ever heard of a few months back," Guzik said. He was friendly now that I was going along with him. "This girl rented a box over at Chemical Bank, and she paid her eight bucks for a year, and she was visiting the box three or four times a day. Always with a guy, always a different guy. So the bank got suspicious and asked us to check it out, and wouldn't you know, the chick is a pross. Instead of taking a hotel room for ten bucks, she's picking up her tricks on the street and taking them to the fucking bank, for Christ's sake. Then she gets her box out and they show her to the little room, and she locks the door and gives the guy a quick blow job in complete privacy, and then she sticks the money in the box and locks it up again. And all it runs her is eight bucks for the year instead of ten bucks a trick, and it's safer than a hotel because if she gets a crazy he's not going to try beating her up in the middle of a fucking bank, is he? She can't get beaten up and she can't get robbed, and it's perfect."

By this time the guard had used his key and mine to get the box from the vault. He handed it to me and led us to a cubicle. We entered together, and Guzik closed and locked the door. The room struck me as rather cramped for sex, but I understand people do it in airplane lavatories, and this was spacious in comparison.

I asked Guzik what had happened to the girl.

"Oh, we told the bank not to press charges, or all it would do was give every streetwalker in the business the same idea. We told them to refund her box-rental fee and tell her they didn't want her business, so I guess that's what they did. She probably walked across the street and started doing business with another bank."

"But you never got any more complaints."

"No. Maybe she's got a friend at Chase Manhattan." He laughed hard at his own line, then chopped it off abruptly. "Let's see what's in the box, Scudder."

I handed it to him. "Open it yourself," I said.

He did, and I watched his face while he looked through everything. He had some interesting comments on the pictures he saw, and he gave the written material a fairly careful reading. Then he looked up suddenly.

"This is all the stuff on the Ethridge dame."

"Seems that way," I said.

"What about the others?"'

"I guess these safe-deposit vaults aren't as foolproof as they're supposed to be. Somebody must have come in and taken everything else."

"You son of a bitch."

"You've got everything you need, Guzik. No more and no less."

"You took a different box for each one. How many others are there?"

"What difference does it make?"

"You son of a bitch. So we'll walk back and ask the guard how many other boxes you have here, and we'll take a look at all of them."

"If you want. I can save you a little time."

"Oh?"

"Not just three different boxes, Guzik. Three different banks. And don't even think about shaking me for the other keys, or running a check on the banks, or anything else you might have in mind. In fact, it might be a good idea if you stopped calling me a son of a bitch, because I might get unhappy, and I might decide not to cooperate in your investigation. I don't have to cooperate, you know. And if I don't, your case goes down the drain. You can possibly tie Ethridge to Lundgren without me, but you'll have a hell of a time finding anything a D.A. is going to want to take to court."

We looked at each other for a while. A couple of times he started to say something, and a couple of times he figured out that it wasn't a particularly good idea. Finally something changed in his face, and I knew he'd decided to let it go. He had enough, and he had all he was going to get, and his face said he knew it.

"The hell," he said, "it's the cop in me, I want to get to the bottom of things. No offense, I hope."

"None at all," I said. I don't suppose I sounded very convincing.

"They probably hauled Ethridge out of bed by now. I'll get back and see what she's got to say. It should make good listening. Or maybe they didn't haul her out of bed. These pictures, you'd have more fun hauling her into bed than out. Ever get any of that, Scudder?"

"No."

"I wouldn't mind a taste myself. Want to come back to the station house with me?"

I didn't want to go anywhere with him. I didn't want to see Beverly Ethridge.

"I'll pass," I said. "I've got an appointment."

CHAPTER SEVENTEEN

I spent half an hour under the shower with the spray as hot as I could stand it. It had been a long night, and the only sleep I'd had had been when I dozed off briefly in Birnbaum's chair. I had come close to being killed, and I had killed the man who'd been trying for me. The Marlboro man, John Michael Lundgren. He'd have been thirty-one next month. I would have guessed him at younger than that, twenty-six or so. Of course, I'd never seen him in particularly good light.

It didn't bother me that he was dead. He had been trying to kill me and had seemed pleased at the prospect. He had killed Spinner, and it wasn't unlikely that he'd killed other people before. He might not have been a pro at killing, but it seemed to be something he enjoyed. He certainly liked working with the knife, and the boys who like to use knives usually get a sexual thrill out of their weaponry. Edged weapons are even more phallic that guns.

I wondered if he'd used a knife on Spinner. It wasn't inconceivably. The Medical Examiner's office doesn't catch everything. There was a case a while

ago, a then-unidentified floater they fished out of the
Hudson, and she was processed and buried without
anyone's noticing that there was a bullet in her skull.
They found out only because some yoyo severed her
head before burial. He wanted the skull for a desk
ornament, and ultimately they found the bullet and
identified the skull from dental records and found
out the woman had been missing from her home in
Jersey for a couple of months.

I let my mind wander with all these thoughts
because there were other thoughts I wanted to avoid,
but after half an hour I turned off the shower and
toweled myself off and picked up the phone and told
them to hold my calls, and to put me down for a
wake-up call at one sharp.

Not that I expected to need the call, because I knew
I wasn't going to be able to sleep. All I could do was
stretch out on the bed and close my eyes and think
about Henry Prager and how I had murdered him.

Henry Prager.

John Lundgren was dead and I had killed him, had
broken his neck, and it did not bother me at all,
because he had done everything possible to earn that
death. And Beverly Ethridge was being grilled by the
police, and it was very possible that they would wind
up with enough on her to put her away for a couple
of years. It was also possible that she would beat it,
because there probably wasn't all that much of a
case, but either way it didn't matter much, because
Spinner would have his vengeance. She could forget
about her marriage and her social position and
cocktails at the Pierre. She could forget about most
of her life, and that didn't bother me either, because
it was nothing she didn't deserve.

But Henry Prager had never killed anybody, and I had pressured him enough to make him blow his brains out, and there was really no way I could justify that. It had bothered me enough when I'd believed him guilty of murder. Now I knew he was innocent, and it bothered me infinitely more.

Oh, there were ways to rationalize it. Evidently his business had turned sour. Evidently he had made a lot of bad financial judgments recently. Evidently he had been up against several different kinds of walls, and evidently he had been a marginal manic-depressive with suicidal tendencies, and that was all well and good, but I had put extra pressure on a man who was in no position to handle it and that had been the last straw, and there was no rationalizing my way out of that one, because it was more than coincidence that he had picked my visit to his office to put the gun in his mouth and pull the trigger.

I lay there with my eyes closed and I wanted a drink. I wanted a drink very badly.

But not yet. Not until I kept my appointment and told an up-and-coming young pederast that he didn't have to pay me a hundred thousand dollars, and that if he could just fool enough of the people enough of the time he could go right ahead and be governor.

By the time I was done talking to him, I had the feeling he might not make bad governor at that. He must have realized the minute I sat down across the desk from him that it would be to his advantage to listen to what I had to say without interrupting. What I had to say must have come as a complete surprise to him, but he just sat there looking absorbed, listening intently, nodding from time to time as a way of punctuating my sentences for me. I told him that he was off

the hook, that he had never really been on it, that it
had all been a device designed to trap a killer without
washing other people's dirty laundry in public. I took
my time telling him, because I wanted to get it all said
on the first try.

When I was done, he leaned back in his chair and
looked at the ceiling. Then he turned his eyes to meet
mine and said his first word.

"Extraordinary."

"I had to pressure you the same as I had to pressure everyone else," I said. "I didn't like it, but it
was what I had to do."

"Oh, I wasn't even feeling all that much pressure,
Mr. Scudder. I recognized that you were a reasonable
sort of man and that it was only a question of raising
the money, a task which did not seem by any means
impossible." He folded his hands on the desk top.
"It's hard for me to digest all of this at once. You
were quite the perfect blackmailer, you know. And
now it seems you were never a blackmailer at all. I've
never been more pleased at being gulled. And the,
uh, photographs—"

"They've all been destroyed."

"I'm to take your word for that, I take it. But isn't
that a silly objection? I'm still thinking of you as a
blackmailer, and that's absurd. If you were a blackmailer, I'd still have to take your word that you
hadn't retained copies of the pictures, it would
always come to that in the end, but since you haven't
extorted money from me to begin with, I can hardly
worry that you will do so in the future, can I?"

"I thought of bringing you the pictures. I also
figured I might get hit by a bus on the way over here,
or leave the envelope in a cab." Spinner, I thought,

had worried about getting hit by a bus. "It seemed simpler to burn them."

"I assure you, I had no desire to see them. Just the knowledge that they cease to exist, that's all I need to feel very much better about things." His eyes probed mine. "You took an awful chance, didn't you? You could have been killed."

"I almost was. Twice."

"I can't understand why you put yourself on the spot like that."

"I'm not sure I understand it myself. Let's say I was doing a favor for a friend."

"A friend?"

"Spinner Jablon."

"An odd sort of person for you to select as a friend, don't you think?"

I shrugged.

"Well, I don't suppose your motives matter very much. You certainly succeeded admirably."

I wasn't so sure of that.

"When you first suggested that you might be able to get those photographs of me, you couched a blackmail demand in terms of a reward. Rather a nice touch, actually." He smiled. "I do think you deserve a reward, however. Perhaps not a hundred thousand dollars, but something substantial, I should say. I don't have much cash on me at the moment—"

"A check will be fine."

"Oh?" He looked at me for a moment, then opened a drawer and took out a checkbook, the large sort with three checks to the page. He uncapped a pen, filled in the date, and looked up at me.

"Can you suggest an amount?"

"Ten thousand dollars," I said.

"It didn't take you long to think of a figure."

"It's a tenth of what you were prepared to pay a blackmailer. It seems a reasonable figure."

"Not unreasonable, and a bargain from my point of view. Shall I make it out to cash or to you personally?"

"Neither."

"Pardon me?"

It wasn't my province to pardon him. I said, "I don't want any money for myself. Spinner hired me and paid me well enough for my time."

"Then—"

"Make it payable to Boys Town. Father Flanagan's Boys Town. I think it's in Nebraska, isn't it?"

He put the pen down and stared at me. His face reddened slightly, and then either he saw the humor in it or the politician in him took over, because he put his head back and laughed. It was a pretty good laugh. I don't know if he meant it or not, but it certainly sounded authentic.

He made out the check and handed it to me. He told me I had a marvelous sense of poetic justice. I folded the check and put it in my pocket.

He said, "Boys Town indeed. You know, Scudder, that's all very much in the past. The subject of those photographs. It was a weakness, a very disabling and unfortunate weakness, but it's all in the past."

"If you say so."

"As a matter of fact, even the desire is completely over and done with, the particular demon exorcised. Even if it were not, I would have no difficulty in resisting the impulse. I have a career that's far too important for me to place in it jeopardy. And these past few months I have truly learned the meaning of jeopardy."

I didn't say anything. He got up and walked around a little and told me all the plans he had for the great State of New York. I didn't pay too much attention. I just listened to the tone, and I decided I believed he was sincere enough. He really wanted to be governor, that was always obvious, but he seemed to want to be governor for reasonably good reasons.

"Well," he said at length, "I seemed to have found an opportunity to make a speech, haven't I? Will I be able to count on your vote. Scudder?"

"No."

"Oh? I thought that was rather a good speech."

"I won't vote against you, either. I don't vote."

"Your duty as a citizen, Mr. Scudder."

"I'm a rotten citizen."

He smiled broadly at that, for reasons that escaped me. "You know," he said, "I like your style, Scudder. For all the bad moments you gave me, I still like your style. I even liked it before I knew the blackmail pose was a charade." He lowered his voice confidentially. "I could find a very good place for someone like you in my organization."

"I'm not interested in organizations. I was in one for fifteen years."

"The Police Department."

"That's right."

"Perhaps I stated it poorly. You wouldn't be part of an organization per se. You'd be working for me."

"I don't like to work for people."

"You're contented with your life as it is."

"Not particularly."

"But you don't want to change it."

"No."

"It's your life," he said. "I'm surprised, though. You have a great deal of depth to you. I should think you would want to accomplish more in the world. I would think you would be more ambitious, if not for your own person advancement then in terms of your potential for doing some good in the world.''

''I told you I was a rotten citizen.''

''Because you don't exercise your right to vote, yes. But I would think— Well, if you should change your mind, Mr. Scudder, the offer will hold.''

I got to my feet. He stood and extended his hand. I didn't really want to shake hands with him, but I couldn't see how to avoid it. His grip was firm and sure, which boded well for him. He was going to have to shake a lot of hands if he wanted to win elections.

I wondered if he'd really lost his passion for young boys. It didn't matter much to me one way or the other. The photos I'd seen had turned my stomach, but I don't know that I had all that much moral objection to them. The boy who'd posed for them had been paid, and undoubtedly knew what he was doing. I didn't like shaking hands with him, and he would never be my choice for a drinking buddy, but I figured he wouldn't be too much worse in Albany than any other son of a bitch who would want the job.

CHAPTER EIGHTEEN

It was around three when I left Huysendahl's office. I thought of calling Guzik and finding out how they were doing with Beverly Ethridge, but I decided to save a dime. I didn't want to talk to him, and I didn't much care how they were doing anyway. I walked around for a while and stopped at a lunch counter on Warren Street. I didn't have an appetite, but it had been a while since I'd had anything to eat, and my stomach was starting to tell me I was mistreating it. I had a couple of sandwiches and some coffee.

I walked around some more. I'd wanted to go to the bank where the data on Henry Prager was tucked away, but it was too late now, they were closed. I decided I'd do that in the morning so that I could destroy all that material. Prager couldn't be hurt any more, but there was still the daughter, and I would feel better when the stuff Spinner had willed to me had ceased to exist.

After a while I got on the subway, and got off at Columbus Circle. There was a message for me at the hotel desk. Anita had called and wanted me to call her back.

I went upstairs and addressed a plain white envelope to Boys Town. I enclosed Huysendahl's check, put a stamp on the envelope, and, in a monumental expression of faith, dropped the letter in the hotel's mail chute. Back in my room, I counted the money I'd taken from the Marlboro man. It came to two hundred and eighty dollars. Some church or other had twenty-eight dollars coming, but at the moment I didn't feel like going to a church. I didn't really feel like much of anything.

It was over now. There was really nothing more to do, and all I felt was empty. If Beverly Ethridge ever stood trial, I would probably have to testify, but that wouldn't be for months, if ever, and the prospect of testifying didn't bother me. I'd given testimony on enough occasions in the past. There was nothing more to do. Huysendahl was free to become governor or not, depending upon the whims of political bosses and the public at large, and Beverly Ethridge was up against the wall, and Henry Prager was going to be buried in a day or so. The moving finger had written and he had written himself off, and my role in his life was as finished as his life itself. He was another person to light meaningless candles for, that was all.

I called Anita.

"Thanks for the money order," she said. "I appreciated it."

"I'd say there's more where that came from," I said. "Except there isn't."

"Are you all right?"

"Sure. Why?"

"You sound different. I don't know how exactly, but you sound different."

"It's been a long week."

There was a pause. Our conversations are usually marked by pauses. Then she said, "The boys were wondering if you wanted to take them to a basket-ball game.''

"In Boston?"

"Pardon me?"

"The Knicks are out of it. The Celtics destroyed them a couple of nights ago. It was the highlight of my week."

"The Nets," she said.

"Oh."

"I think they're in the finals. Against Utah or something."

"Oh." I can never remember that New York has a second basketball team. I don't know why. I've taken my sons to the Nassau Coliseum to watch the Nets and I still tend to forget they exist. "When are they playing?"

"There's a home game Saturday night."

"What's today?"

"Are you serious?"

"Look, I'll get a calendar watch next time I think of it. What's today?"

"Thursday."

"Tickets will probably be hard to get."

"Oh, they're all sold out. They thought you might know somebody."

I thought of Huysendahl. He could probably swing tickets without much trouble. He would also prob-ably have enjoyed meeting my sons. Of course, there were enough other people who could manage to ob-tain last-minute tickets, and who wouldn't mind do-ing me a favor.

I said, "I don't know. It's cutting it kind of close." But what I was thinking was that I didn't want to see my sons, not in just two days' time, and I didn't know why. And I was also wondering if they really wanted me to take them to the game or if they simply wanted to go to it and knew that I would be able to root out a source of tickets.

I asked if there were any other home games.

"Thursday. But that's a school night."

"It's also a lot more possible than Saturday."

"Well, I hate to see them stay out late on a school night."

"I could probably get tickets for the Thursday game."

"Well—"

"I couldn't get tickets for Saturday, but I could probably get something for Thursday. It'll be later in the series, a more important game."

"Oh, so that's the way you want to do it. If I say no because it's a school night, then I'm the heavy."

"I think I'll hang up."

"No, don't do that. All right, Thursday is fine. You'll call if you can get tickets?"

I said I would.

It was odd—I wanted to be drunk but didn't much want a drink. I sat around the room for a while, then walked over to the park and sat on a bench. A couple of kids ambled rather purposefully to a bench nearby. They sat down and lit cigarettes, and then one of them noticed me and nudged his companion, who looked carefully toward me. They got up and walked off, glancing back periodically to make sure I was not following them. I stayed where I was. I guessed that one of them had been about to sell drugs to the other, and that they had looked at me and decided not to conduct the transaction under the eyes of someone who looked like a policeman.

I don't know how long I sat there. A couple of hours, I suppose. Periodically a panhandler would brace me. Sometimes I'd contribute toward the next bottle of sweet wine. Sometimes I'd tell the bum to fuck off.

By the time I left the park and walked over to Ninth Avenue, St. Paul's was closed for the day. The downstairs was opening up, however. It was too late to pray but just the right hour for bingo.

Armstrong's was open, and it had been a long dry night and day. I told them to forget the coffee.

The next forty hours or so were pretty much of a blur. I don't know how long I stayed in Armstrong's or where I went after that. Sometime Friday morning I woke up alone in a hotel room in the Forties, a squalid room in the kind of hotel to which Times Square streetwalkers take their johns. I had no memory of a woman and my money was all still there, so it looked as though I had probably checked in alone. There was a pint bottle of bourbon on the dresser, about two-thirds empty. I killed it and left the hotel and went on drinking, and reality faded in and out, and sometime during that night I must have decided I was done, because I managed to find my way back to my hotel.

Saturday morning the telephone woke me. It seemed to ring for a long time before I roused myself enough to reach for it. I managed to knock it off the little nightstand and onto the floor, and by the time I managed to pick it up and get it to my ear I was reasonably close to consciousness.

It was Guzik.

"You're hard to find," he said. "I been trying to reach you since yesterday. Didn't you get my messages?"

"I didn't stop at the desk."

"I gotta talk to you."

"What about?"

"When I see you. I'll be over in ten minutes."

I told him to give me half an hour. He said he'd meet me in the lobby. I said that would be fine.

I stood under the shower, first hot, then cold. I took a couple of aspirin and drank a lot of water. I had a hangover, which I had certainly earned, but aside from that I felt reasonably good. The drinking had purged me. I would still carry Henry Prager's death around with me—you cannot entirely shrug off such burdens—but I had managed to drown some of the guilt, and it was no longer as oppressive as it had been.

I took the clothes I'd been wearing, wadded them up, and stuffed them into the closet. Eventually I'd decide whether the cleaner could restore them, but for the moment I didn't even want to think about it. I shaved and put on clean clothes and drank two more glasses of tap water. The aspirin had polished off the headache, but I was dehydrated from too many hours of hard drinking, and every cell in my body had an unquenchable thirst.

I got down to the lobby before he arrived. I checked the desk and found that he'd called four times. There were no other messages, and no mail of any importance. I was reading one of the unimportant letters—an insurance company would give me a leather-covered memorandum book absolutely free if I would tell my date of birth—when Guzik came in. He was wearing a well-tailored suit; you had to look carefully to see he was carrying a gun.

He came over and took a chair next to me. He told me again that I was hard to find. "Wanted to talk to you after I saw Ethridge," he said. "Jesus, she's something, isn't she? She turns the class on and off. One minute you can't believe she was ever a pross, and the next minute you can't believe she was anything else but.''

"She's an odd one, all right.''

"Uh-huh. She's also getting out sometime today.''

"She made bail? I thought they'd book her for Murder One.''

"Not bail. Not booking her for anything, Matt. We got nothing to hold her on.''

I looked at him. I could feel the muscles in my forearms tightening. I said, "How much did it cost her?''

"I told you, no bail. We—''

"What did it cost her to buy out of a murder charge? I always heard you could wash homicide if you had enough cash. Never saw it done, but I heard about it, and—''

He was almost ready to swing, and I was by God hoping he would do it, because I wanted an excuse to put him through the wall. A tendon stood out on his neck, and his eyes narrowed to slits. Then he relaxed suddenly, and his face regained its original color.

He said, "Well, you would have to figure it that way, wouldn't you?''

"Well?''

He shook his head. "Nothing to hold her on,'' he said again. "That's what I was trying to tell you.''

"How about Spinner Jablon?''

"She didn't kill him.''

"Her bully boy did. Her pimp, whatever the hell he was. Lundgren.''

"No way.''

"The hell.''

"No way,'' Guzik said. "He was in California. Town called Santa Paula, it's halfway between L.A. and Santa Barbara.''

''He flew here and then flew back.''

''No way. He was there from a few weeks before we fished Spinner out of the river until a couple of days afterward, and nobody's gonna shake that alibi. He did thirty days in Santa Paula city jail. They tagged him for assault and let him plead to drunk and disorderly. He did the whole thirty days. Just no way on earth that he was in New York when Spinner got it.''

I stared at him.

''So maybe she had another boyfriend,'' he went on. ''We figured that was possible. We could try to turn him up, but does it make any sense that way? She wouldn't use one guy to hit Spinner and another to go after you. It doesn't make sense.''

''What about the assault on me?''

''What about it?'' He shrugged. ''Maybe she put him up to it. Maybe she didn't. She swears she didn't. Her story is she called him for advice when you put the screws to her and he flew out to see if he could help. She said she told him not to get rough, that she thought she would be able to buy you off. That's her story, but what can you expect her to say? Maybe she wanted him to kill you and maybe she didn't, but how can you put enough together to make a case out of it? Lundgren is dead, and nobody else has any information that absolutely implicates her. There's no evidence to tie her to the attack on you. You can prove she knew Lundgren and you can prove she had a motive for wanting you dead. You can't prove any kind of an accessory or conspiracy charge. You can't come up with anything to get an indictment returned, you can't even get anything that would make anybody in the District Attorney's office take the whole thing seriously.''

"There's no way the Santa Paula records are wrong?"

"No way. Spinner would have had to spend a month in the river, and it didn't happen that way."

"No. He was alive within ten days of the time the body was found. I spoke to him on the telephone. I don't get it. She had to have another accomplice."

"Maybe. Polygraph says no."

"She agreed to take a lie-detector test?"

"We never asked her to. She demanded it. It gets her completely off the hook as far as Spinner was concerned. It's not quite as clear as far as the attack on you was concerned. The expert who administered the test says there's a little stress involved, that his guess would be she did and didn't know Lundgren was going to try to take you out. Like she suspected it but they hadn't talked about it and she'd been able to avoid thinking about it."

"Those tests aren't always a hundred percent."

"They come close enough, Matt. Sometimes they'll make a person look guilty when he's not, especially if the operator isn't very good at what he's doing. But if they say you're innocent, it's a pretty good bet you are. I think they ought to be admissible in court."

I had always felt that way myself. I sat there for a while trying to run it all through my mind until everything fell into place. It took its time. Meanwhile, Guzik went on talking about the interrogation of Beverly Ethridge, pointing up his remarks with observations on what he would like to do with her. I didn't pay him much attention.

I said, "The car wasn't him. I should have realized that."

"How's that?"

"The car," I said. "I told you a car took a shot at

me one night. The same night I spotted Lundgren for
the first time, and the place was the same as where he
came at me with the knife, so I had to think it was the
same man both times.''

''You never saw the driver?''

''No. I figured it was Lundgren because he'd been
dogging me earlier that night and I thought he'd been
setting me up. But it couldn't have been that way. It
wouldn't be his style. He liked that knife too much.''

''Then who was it?''

''Spinner said somebody ran up onto a curb after
him. The same bit.''

''Who?''

''Plus the voice on the phone. Then there were no
calls any more.''

''I don't follow you, Matt.''

I looked at him. ''Trying to make the pieces fit.
That's all. Somebody killed Spinner.''

''The question is who.''

I nodded. ''That's the question,'' I said.

''One of the other people he gave you the dope
on?''

''They all check out,'' I said. ''Maybe he had more
people after him than he ever told me about. Maybe
he added somebody to the string after he gave me the
envelope. The hell, maybe somebody rolled him for
his cash, hit him too hard, panicked, and threw the
body in the river.''

''It happens.''

''Sure it happens.''

''You think we'll ever find out who did him?''

I shook my head. ''Do you?''

''No,'' Guzik said. ''No, I don't think we ever
will.''

CHAPTER NINETEEN

I had never been in the building before. There were two doormen on duty, and the elevator was manned. The doormen made sure that I was expected, and the elevator operator whisked me up eighteen floors and indicated which door was the one I was looking for. He didn't budge until I had rung the bell and been admitted.

The apartment was as impressive as the rest of the building. There was a stairway leading to a second floor. An olive-skinned maid led me into a large den with oak-paneled walls and a fireplace. About half the books on the shelves were bound in leather. It was a very comfortable room in a very spacious apartment. The apartment had cost almost two hundred thousand dollars, and the monthly maintenance charge came to something like fifteen hundred.

When you've got enough money, you can buy just about anything you want.

"He will be with you in a moment," the maid said. "He said for you to help yourself to a drink."

She pointed to a serving bar alongside the fireplace. There was ice in a silver bucket, and a couple of dozen bottles. I sat in a red leather chair and waited for him.

I didn't have to wait very long. He entered the room. He was wearing white flannel slacks and a plaid blazer. He had a pair of leather house slippers on his feet.

"Well, now," he said. He smiled to show how genuinely glad he was to see me. "You'll have something to drink, I hope."

"Not just now."

"It's a little early for me too, as a matter of fact. You sounded quite urgent on the phone, Mr. Scudder. I gather you've had second thoughts about working for me."

"No."

"I received the impression—"

"That was to get in here."

He frowned. "I'm not sure I understand."

"I'm really not sure whether you do or not, Mr. Huysendahl. I think you'd better close the door."

"I don't care for your tone."

"You're not going to care for any of this," I said. "You'll like it less with the door open. I think you should close it."

He was about to say something, perhaps another observation about my tone of voice and how little he cared for it, but instead he closed the door.

"Sit down, Mr. Huysendahl."

He was used to giving orders, not taking them, and I thought he was going to make an issue out of it. But he sat down, and his face wasn't quite enough of a mask to keep me from knowing that he knew what it was all about. I'd known anyway, because there was just no other way the pieces could fit together, but his face confirmed it for me.

"Are you going to tell me what this is all about?"

"Oh, I'm going to tell you. But I think you already know. Don't you?"

"Certainly not."

I looked over his shoulder at an oil painting of somebody's ancestor. Maybe one of his. I didn't notice any family resemblance, though.

I said, "You killed Spinner Jablon."

"You're out of your mind."

"No."

"You already found out who killed Jablon. You told me that the day before yesterday."

"I was wrong."

"I don't know what you're driving at, Scudder—"

"A man tried to kill me Wednesday night," I said. "You know about that. I assumed he was the same man who killed Spinner, and I managed to tie him to one of Spinner's other suckers, so I thought that cleared you. But it turns out that he couldn't have killed Spinner, because he was on the other side of the country at the time. His alibi for Spinner's death was as solid as they come. He was in jail at the time."

I looked at him. He was patient now, hearing me out with the same intent stare he had fixed on me Thursday afternoon when I told him he was in the clear.

I said, "I should have known he wasn't the only one involved, that more than one of Spinner's victims had decided to fight back. The man who tried to kill me was a loner. He liked to use a knife. But I'd been attacked earlier by one or more men in a car, a stolen car. And a few minutes after that attack I had a phone call from an older man with a New York accent. I'd had a call from that man before. It didn't make sense that the knife artist would have had anybody else in on it. So somebody else was behind the dodge with the car, and somebody else was responsible for knocking Spinner on the head and dumping him in the river.''

"That doesn't mean I had anything to do with it.''

"I think it does. As soon as the man with the knife is taken out of the picture, it's obvious that everything was pointing to you all along. He was an amateur, but in other respects the operation was all quite professional. A car stolen from another neighborhood with a very good man at the wheel. Some men who were good enough to find Spinner when he didn't want to be found. You had the money to hire that kind of talent. And you had the connections.''

"That's nonsense.''

"No," I said. "I've been thinking about it. One thing that threw me was your reaction when I first came to your office. You didn't know Spinner was dead until I showed you the item in the paper. I almost ruled you out, because I couldn't believe you could fake a reaction that well. But of course it wasn't a fake. You really didn't know he was dead, did you?''

"Of course not." He drew his shoulders back. "And I think that's fairly good evidence that I had nothing to do with his death.''

I shook my head. "It just means you didn't know about it yet. And you were stunned by the realization both that Spinner was dead and that the whole game didn't end with his death. I not only had the evidence on you, I also knew you were tied to Spinner and a possible suspect in his death. Naturally that shook you up a little.''

"You can't prove anything. You can say that I hired someone to kill Spinner. I didn't, and I can swear to you that I didn't, but it's hardly something I can prove either. But the point is that it's not incumbent upon me to prove it, is it?''

"No.''

"And you can accuse me of whatever you want, but you don't have a shred of proof either, do you?"

"No, I don't."

"Then perhaps you'll tell me why you decided to come here this afternoon, Mr. Scudder."

"I don't have proof. That's true. But I have something else, Mr. Huysendahl."

"Oh?"

"I have those photographs."

He gaped. "You distinctly told me—"

"That I had burned them."

"Yes."

"I'd intended to. It was simpler to tell you it had already been done. I've been busy since then, and didn't get around to it. And then this morning I found out that the man with the knife was not the man who killed Spinner, and I sifted through some of the things that I already knew, and I saw that it had to be you. So it was just as well that I didn't burn those pictures, wasn't it?"

He got slowly to his feet. "I think I'll have that drink after all," he said.

"Go right ahead."

"Will you join me?"

"No."

He put ice cubes in a tall glass, poured Scotch, added soda from a siphon. He took his time building the drink, then walked over to the fireplace and rested with his elbow on the burnished oak mantel. He took a few small sips of his drink before he turned to look at me again.

"Then we're back to the beginning," he said. "And you've decided to blackmail me."

"No."

"Why else is it so fortunate for you that you didn't burn the pictures?"

"Because it's the only hold I've got on you."

"And what are you going to do with it?"

"Nothing."

"Then—"

"It's what you're going to do, Mr. Huysendahl."

"And what am I going to do?"

"You're not going to run for governor."

He stared at me. I didn't really want to look at his eyes, but I forced myself. He was no longer trying to keep his face a mask, and I was able to watch as he tried one one of thought after another and found that none of them led anywhere.

"You've thought this out, Scudder."

"Yes."

"At length, I would suppose."

"Yes."

"And there's nothing you want, is there? Money, power, the things most people want. It wouldn't do any good for me to send another check to Boys Town."

"No."

He nodded. He worried the tip of his chin with a finger. He said, "I don't know who killed Jablon."

"I assumed as much."

"I didn't order him killed."

"The order originated with you. One way or the other, you're the man at the top."

"Probably."

I looked at him.

"I'd prefer to believe otherwise," he said. "When you told me the other day that you'd found the man who killed Jablon, I was enormously relieved. Not because I felt the killing could possibly be attributed to me, that any sort of trail would lead back to me. But because I honestly did not know whether I was in any way responsible for his death."

"You didn't order it directly."

"No, of course not. I didn't want the man killed."

"But somebody in your organization—"

He sighed heavily. "It would seem that someone decided to take matters into his own hands. I . . . confided in several people that I was being blackmailed. It appeared that it might be possible to recover the evidence without acceding to Jablon's demands. More important, it was necessary to devise some way in which Jablon's silence could be purchased on a permanent basis. The trouble with blackmail is that one never ceases to pay it. The cycle can go on forever, there's no control."

"So somebody tried to scare Spinner once with a car."

"So it would seem."

"And when that didn't work, somebody hired somebody to hire somebody to kill him."

"I suppose so. You can't prove it. What's perhaps more to the point, *I* can't prove it."

"But you believed it all along, didn't you? Because you warned me that one payment was all I was going to get. And if I tried to tap you again, you'd have me killed."

"Did I really say that?"

"I think you remember saying it, Mr. Huysendahl. I should have seen the significance in that at the time. You were thinking of murder as a weapon in your arsenal. Because you'd already used it once."

"I never intended for a moment that Jablon should die."

I stood up. I said, "I was reading something the other day about Thomas à Becket. He was very close to one of the kings of England. One of the Henrys, I think Henry the Second."

"I believe I see the parallel."

"Do you know the story? When he became Archbishop of Canterbury he stopped being Henry's buddy and played the game according to his conscience. It rattled Henry, and he let some of his underlings know it. 'Oh, that someone might rid me of that rebellious priest!' "

"But he never intended that Thomas be murdered."

"That was his story," I agreed. "His subordinates decided Henry had issued Thomas's death warrant. Henry didn't see it that way at all, he'd just been thinking out loud, and he was very upset to learn that Thomas was dead. Or at least he pretended to be very upset. He's not around, so we can't ask him."

"And you're taking the position that Henry was responsible."

"I'm saying I wouldn't vote for him for governor of New York."

He finished his drink. He put the glass on the bar and sat down in his chair again, crossing one leg over the other.

He said, "If I run for governor—"

"Then every major newspaper in the state gets a full set of those photographs. Until you announce for governor, they stay where they are."

"Where is that?"

"A very safe place."

"And I have no option."

"No."

"No other choice."

"None."

"I might be able to determine the man responsible for Jablon's death."

"Perhaps you could. It's also possible you couldn't. But what good would that do? He's sure to be a professional, and there would be no evidence to link him to either you or Jablon, let alone enough to bring him to trial. And you couldn't do anything with him without exposing yourself.''

"You're making this terribly difficult, Scudder.''

"I'm making it very easy. All you have to do is forget about being governor.''

"I would be an excellent governor. If you're so fond of historical parallels, you might consider Henry the Second a bit further. He's regarded as one of England's better monarchs.''

"I wouldn't know.''

"I would.'' He told me some things about Henry. I gather he knew quite a bit about the subject. It might have been interesting. I didn't pay much attention to it. Then he went on to tell me some more about what a good governor he would make, what he would accomplish for the people of the state.

I cut him short. I said, "You have a lot of plans, but that doesn't mean anything. You wouldn't be a good governor. You won't be any kind of governor, because I'm not going to let you, but you wouldn't be a good one because you're capable of picking people to work for you who are capable of murder. That's enough to disqualify you.''

"I could discharge those people.''

"I couldn't know if you did or not. And the individuals aren't even that important.''

"I see.'' He sighed again. "He wasn't much of a man, you know. I'm not justifying murder when I say that. He was a petty crook and a shoddy blackmailer. He began by entrapping me, preying on a personal weakness, and then he tried to bleed me.''

"He wasn't much of a man at all,'' I agreed.

"Yet his murder is that significant to you.''

"I don't like murder.''

"You believe that human life is sacred, then.''

"I don't know if I believe that anything is sacred. It's a very complicated question. I've taken human life. A few days ago I killed a man. Not long before that, I contributed to a man's death. My contribution was unintentional. That hasn't made me feel all that much better about it. I don't know if human life is sacred. I just don't like murder. And you're in the process of getting away with murder, and that bothers me, and there's just one thing I'm going to do about it. I don't went to kill you, I don't want to expose you, I don't want to do any of those things. I'm sick of playing an incompetent version of God. All I'm going to do is keep you out of Albany."

"Doesn't that constitute playing God?"

"I don't think so."

"You say human life is sacred. Not in so many words, but that seems to be your position. What about my life, Mr. Scudder? For years now only one thing has been important to me, and you're presuming to tell me I can't have it."

I looked around the den. The portraits, the furnishings, the service bar. "It looks to me as though you're doing pretty well," I said.

"I have material possessions. I can afford them."

"Enjoy them."

"Is there no way I can buy you? Are you that devoutly incorruptible?"

"I'm probably corrupt, by most definitions. But you can't buy me, Mr. Huysendahl."

I waited for him to say something. A few minutes went by, and he just remained where he was, silent, his eyes looking off into the middle distance. I found my own way out.

CHAPTER TWENTY

This time I got to St. Paul's before it closed. I stuffed a tenth of what I'd taken from Lundgren into the poor box. I lit a few candles for various dead people who came to mind. I sat for a while and watched people take their turns in the confessional. I decided that I envied them, but not enough to do anything about it.

I went across the street to Armstrong's and had a plate of beans and sausage, then a drink and a cup of coffee. It was over now, it was all over, and I could drink normally again, never getting drunk, never staying entirely sober. I nodded at people now and then, and some of them nodded back to me. It was Saturday, so Trina was off, but Larry did just as good a job of bringing more coffee and bourbon when my cup was empty.

Most of the time I just let my mind wander, but from time to time I would find myself going over the events since Spinner had walked in and given me his envelope. There were probably ways I could have handled things better. If I'd pushed it a little and taken an interest at the beginning, I might even have been able to keep Spinner alive. But it was over and I was done with it, and I even had some of his money left after what I'd paid to Anita and the churches and various bartenders, and I could relax now.

"This seat taken?"

I hadn't even noticed when she came in. I looked up and there she was. She sat down across from me and took a pack of cigarettes from her bag. She shook a cigarette loose and lit it.

I said, "You're wearing the white pants suit."

"That's so you'll be able to recognize me. You sure managed to turn my life inside out, Matt."

"I guess I did. They're not going to press anything, are they?"

"They couldn't press a pants suit, let alone a charge. Johnny never knew Spinner existed. That should be my biggest headache."

"You've got other headaches?"

"In a manner of speaking, I just got rid of a headache. It cost me a lot to get rid of him, though."

"Your husband?"

She nodded. "He decided without too much trouble that I was a luxury he intended to deny himself. He's getting a divorce. And I am not getting any alimony, because if I give him any trouble he's going to give me ten times as much trouble, and I think he'd probably do it. Not that there wasn't enough shit in the papers already, as far as that goes."

"I haven't been keeping up with the papers."

"You've missed some nice stuff." She drew on her cigarette and blew out a cloud of smoke. "You really do your drinking in all the class joints, don't you? I tried your hotel but you weren't in, so then I tried Polly's Cage, and they said you came here a lot of the time. I can't imagine why."

"It suits me."

She cocked her head, studying me. "You know something? It does. But me a drink?"

"Sure."

I got Larry's attention, and she ordered a glass of wine. "It probably won't be terrific," she said, "but at least it's hard for the bartender to fuck it up." When he brought it she raised her glass to me, and I returned the gesture with my cup. "Happy days," she said.

"Happy days."

"I didn't want him to kill you, Matt."

"Neither did I."

"I'm serious. All I wanted was time. I would have handled everything on my own, one way or another. I never called Johnny, you know. How would I have known how to reach him? He called me after he got out of jail. He wanted me to send him some money. He would do that now and then, when he was up against it. I felt guilty about turning state's evidence that time, even though it had been his idea. But when I had him on the phone I couldn't keep myself from telling him I was in trouble, and that was a mistake. He was more trouble than I was ever in."

"What was the hold he had on you?"

"I don't know. But he always had it."

"You fingered me for him. That night at Polly's."

"He wanted to get a look at you."

"He got it. Then I set up a meeting with you Wednesday. The cute thing about that was I wanted to tell you you were clear. I thought I already had the killer, and I wanted to let you know the blackmail routine was over and done with. Instead, you put off the meeting for a day and sent him after me."

"He was going to talk to you. Scare you off, stall for time, something like that."

"That's not the way he saw it. You must have

figured he'd try what he tried.''

She hesitated for a moment, then let her shoulders drop. ''I knew it was possible. He was . . . he had a wildness in him.'' Her face brightened suddenly, and something danced in her eyes. ''Maybe you did me a favor,'' she said. ''Maybe I'm a lot better off with him out of my life.''

''Better off than you know.''

''What do you mean?''

''I mean there was a very good reason why he wanted me dead. I'm just guessing, but I like my guesses. You would have been happy to stall me until you came into some money, which would happen once Kermit came into the principal of his inheritance. But Lundgren couldn't afford to have me around, now or later. Because he had big plans for you.''

''What do you mean?''

''Can't you guess? He probably told you he'd have you divorce Ethridge once he'd come into enough money to make it worthwhile.''

''How did you know?''

''I told you. Just a guess. But I don't think he'd have done it that way. He would have wanted the whole thing. He'd have waited until your husband inherited his money, and then he would have taken his time setting it up right, and all of a sudden you'd turn out to be a very rich widow.''

''Oh, God.''

''Then you'd remarry and your name would be Beverly Lundgren. How long do you suppose it would have taken him to put another notch on his knife.''

''God!''

''Of course, it's just a guess.''

"No." She shivered, and all of a sudden her face lost a lot of its polish and she looked like the girl she had stopped being a long time ago. "He'd have done it just that way," she said. "It's more than a guess. That's just the way he would have done it."

"Another glass of wine?"

"No." She put her hand on mine. "I was all primed to be mad at you for turning my life around. Maybe that's not all you did. Maybe you saved it."

"We'll never know, will we?"

"No." She crushed out her cigarette. She said, "Well, where do I go from here? I was beginning to get used to a life of leisure, Matt. I thought I carried it off with a certain flair."

"That you did."

"Now all of a sudden I've got to find a way to make a living."

"You'll think of something, Beverly."

Her eyes focused on mine. She said, "That's the first time you used my name, do you know that?"

"I know."

We sat there for a while looking at each other. She reached for a cigarette, changed her mind, and pushed it back in the pack. "Well, what do you know," she said.

"I didn't say anything.

"I thought I didn't do a thing for you. I was beginning to worry that I was losing my touch. Is there some place we can go? I'm afraid my place isn't my place any more."

"There's my hotel."

"You take me to all the class joints," she said. She got to her feet and picked up her bag. "Let's go. Right now, huh?"